To Dance or Not to Dance?
This is Not the Question.

A Novel
Based on the Life of
Indian Entertainer
Haleem Khan
by
L.R.Johnson

Pharos Books

©Publishers

Publisher: Pharos Books (P) Ltd.
Plot No.-55, Main Mother Dairy Road
Pandav Nagar, East Delhi-110092
Phone: 011-40395855, +14049995474
WhatsApp: +91 8368220032
E-mail: sales@pharosbooks.in
Website: www.pharosbooks.in
Edition: 2022

Printed By: Sushma Book Binding House, Okhla
Industrial Area, Phase II, New Delhi-110020

To Dance or Not to Dance? This is Not the Question

Haleem Khan

Contents

Acknowledgment and Dedications

Firstly, I would like to dedicate this novel to Haleem Khan, his family, and friends. He has travelled a very difficult journey to achieve what he has achieved, and I sincerely hope that this story, based upon his character, helps him further in his personal quest to perform to the world his fabulous talents!

I wish to explain that although the backbone of the story pertains to Haleem's life, it is not a biographical description of Haleem's real-life. The intention is to create a novel/ screenplay based upon fictional non-fictional events surrounding the time from birth to his present status.

Haleem requested me to write in this manner because an actual biography was not his intention. In the following pages, I hope to have created a very interesting; sometimes sad, sometimes happy, emotional, but guaranteed mesmerizing novel/ film script including some truth and some fiction. In fact, a mixed bag that Haleem wishes to use to enhance his already successful stature in the Indian entertainment world, which is growing rapidly throughout the world.

Preface

The story of Haleem begins 32 years ago in his birthplace, Ongole in the Andhra Pradesh State, India. Born into a family consisting of Haleem's mother, Mehetai Begum and father, Rasheed Khan, plus his younger sister. One would think this was quite typical, well it was until Haleem began to realise that he was slightly different than other boys with whom he shared his school years. At a very early age, Haleem was mesmerized by images coming through the family's TV of women performing a traditional, classical historical dance called, Kuchipudi, among other traditional dances that have enriched Indian society ever since the world discovered this most wonderful country.

As a young boy, Haleem, endeavoring to ignore his attraction to the fabulous female dancers, but failing, he secretly, in his bedroom, and away from the skeptical eyes of his parents; would perform dances and copy the movements of these fabulous dancers hoping to become as beautiful and graceful as them. However, there was one major problem, he was a boy, and Indian boys studied hard and played cricket with their friends on the surrounding wastelands of Ongole. Not one of his friends desired to copy or even contemplate being attracted by such a female orientated hobby.

In his early days, Haleem, could control his inner urge to copy female dancers. In fact, he would venture out with his mates and play cricket, happily supported by his father who saw a certain talent in his son. However, the real talent hidden in Haleem's mind and body; his father never would have imagined. He was just happy that his only son was pursuing his studies correctly, playing cricket in his free time and generally doing what all Indian boys loved to do, whack cricket balls until it was too dark to see the ball anymore.

Haleem's parents were quite satisfied with his academic qualities and felt that their son would continue the families' proud traditions of producing children that fitted perfectly into the higher echelons of Indian society.

"What would he become?" They thought? "A lawyer, doctor, scientist, professional entrepreneur, etc.?" The world was his oyster, so they believed as he progressed through the most difficult years all young people must endure, puberty.

Without getting into a psychological dilemma, Haleem managed to control his continuing attraction to the wonderful world of Kuchipudi dancing by concentrating on his studies and pleasing his parents. However, in moments of secrecy, he would play video tapes of Kuchipudi dancers performing in their wonderful, silk and very colorful robes, hoping one day that he would be able to possess such beautiful clothes and perform to a huge public with astonishing make-up and long black eyelashes, just like those of his female 'fantasies', which refused to exit his confused mind.

Like all teenage boys, the teenage years alter, confuse, disturb the minds and bodies of young people, Haleem, realized he was just like other boys who enjoyed his wonderful, gentle company because that is exactly what he was, a quite pleasant young boy. However, slightly different to others.

His inquisitive mind had a sanctuary of peace as he escaped into the fantasy world of his favorite dances, in secrecy of course, hoping that his parents would not discover this urge to dress and dance like a female. He would spend hours and hours in front of the TV or slip off to the local cinema who were showing films of Indian traditional dance, music and Bollywood, in the hope that they would also show parts of the dance he most desired, Kuchipudi.

Somehow, Haleem managed to keep his secret from his parents. He reached an acceptable academic level. So, really there was no need for his parents to probe into his private life because Haleem continued to function as a normal teenage boy. In addition, in India, parental pressure for young males to find female partners was, at this level, not so important, only the very rich and well off would put pressure on their male siblings to marry young females of a higher status. Thus, keeping strict, family traditions going in the hope of connecting to an even richer family through marriage; arranged marriages that is.

Although Haleem's family were of a higher cast, they did not belong to the wealthiest in their town. So, boys like Haleem would be expected to perform well at school hoping for a future in a professional sector, which would eventually bring a higher status and pride to the family.

In addition, the hope that their son would attract the attention of a female from a higher cast, rich family. That is the way it is in India; love in marriage can come later and is secondary if the financial foundations for the future are arranged and organized by speculative parents hoping their sons or daughters will find a suitable partner.

Going through puberty is normally punishment for most kids growing into teenagers. So, one can imagine what it was like for Haleem having this attraction for an effeminate, orientated dance form and attempting to act as 'normal' as possible in front of his parents and family members, especially in a society that tends to reject any divertive orientations, which could bring shame to the family.

Being constantly driven by his inner urge to learn the intricate movements and mannerisms of Kuchipudi dancers whilst avoiding any subversive attention from the family, Haleem developed an extreme method of discipline that enabled him to pursue his 'karma' and act quite 'normal' when required.

Kuchipudi tradition and the demanding training required to perfect the skills of ancient dance routines is comparable to Chinese and Japanese traditional dances. This Haleem also took into his stride after studying movements and gestures of Far Eastern dance routines. I.e., Japanese Kyoto, Kabuki, Noh Mai, Bon Odori, among others influenced Haleem. In addition, Chinese ancient dances including Yangge, Lhamo, a Tibetan traditional dance routine, and of course the popular Lion and Dragon Dances performed all over China in opera houses and open-air traditional processions.

Mesmerized by the fantastic, colorful, exciting dancers dressed in wonderful flowing robes, kimonos, a plethora of beautiful silk costumes and, of course, their make-up; deep down inside his heart, Haleem knew that his destiny would be performing Kuchipudi live, and nothing could stop him.

In the beginning (where better?)

A piercing, agonising scream shatters the calm before the storm as Haleem's mother pushes once more for her life, and Haleem's too. In the small, dusty, very hot, windswept village of Ongole, somewhere in the middle of Andhra Pradesh, a sign of life becomes a thing of massive importance especially a male one. There was no way back, as the midwife stretches her legs even further apart preparing for a grand finale in the battle for life and death twixt a black tunnel and the light of life at the end of it.

"Eureka," she screams (and that was just the midwife) as a beautiful male baby appears with a pair of huge, wonderful brown eyes that greeted the world not quite knowing what the future would hold. At this moment in time the only thoughts of everybody concerned were,

"Is it healthy, what is it, a male or female?" Nothing else matters as long as it is a boy!

"Madam, you have given birth to a wonderful, healthy male child," The midwife assisting in the birth tells the mother who smiles with relief because having a girl as a first child to join the family would be not quite so acceptable.

The midwife passes the beautiful baby over to the mother as a gentle knock on the door splits the heavenly, adoring silence, attainable solely between a new born baby and its mother.

"Darling, what have you produced for the family, I sincerely hope it is a bouncing, healthy boy!" The father says as he enters the room looking rather worried.

"No worries darling, this time we have been blessed with the luck of the gods and here is your inheritor, we'll call him Haleem, the strong one!"

Rasheed Khan, the father, beams from ear-to-ear, rushes over to his rather weary, and still in substantial pain wife, Mehetai Begum, who proudly sits up in her bed holding the newborn baby to her oversized breasts that are waiting to open for one of the most important things in life, a baby's initial feed.

"Darling, I am so proud of you and Haleem, he is wonderful!" Rasheed stands on the side of the bed bursting with excitement hoping to hold his pride and joy for the very first time.

"Not yet darling, Haleem needs his first feed, you will just have to wait your turn!"

The midwife steps in and maneuvers Haleem's mouth towards her succulent, full of nourishment breasts; a moment to remember for the rest of their lives as he does what all baby's instinctually do, he begins to suck!

Rasheed looks down at the happy pair joined for the first time outside of Mehetai's expanded body, but who cares about such minor details if mother, father and baby are unified and, over the moon with ecstatic happiness.

"He's so wonderful and look at those huge brown eyes and eyelashes!" Rasheed says, as tears of joy exit his own expanded eyes; a seldom occurrence in Indian society, but on such a special occasion, even Indian society will accept feelings of emotion.

"Yes, darling he is wonderful now please leave us alone I am feeling very weary, and after Haleem's nine month-long journey, he will need to rest too. So, after I have finished feeding him you can give him a quick hug then you must leave." The midwife nods in agreement as Rasheed gently approaches the side of the bed, kisses his wife, and Haleem, and says,

"I can wait darling; we have all of our lives to show our affections and now I will leave the room to join the others in the family and tell them the great news! However, may I just give Haleem a tiny kiss on his cheek?"

"OK, just one tiny peck and then leave us alone please," Mehetai says.

"Sure," Rasheed replies moving forward gently he kisses Haleem on his cheek careful not to disturb the marvelous, maternal connection taking place before him, then he turns and leaves the room.

After feeding time, and half asleep, the proud new mother Mehetai gently asks the midwife,

"Please take our son and place him in his cot in the next room and let nobody in!"

"Yes madam, I will make sure nobody enters, now please get some rest, you will need it for the coming days and months. Here is a pill to help you rest, and do not worry, precious

Haleem is in safe hands." She replies and removes Haleem, now sleeping, from his mother's welcoming breast then places him in a beautiful, ancient cot, given to the family by the grandparents.

Before the midwife removes the baby from the room, Mehetai, falls into a deep sleep, recovering from a painful experience solely designated for women of the world and, totally underestimated by their male partners, even more so in Asian and African regions.

Chapter Two

The early years

Haleem certainly turns out to be no ordinary baby, toddler, or child. Although the first 6 months of his life were spent like any other normal Muslim baby, especially male ones. Pampered, and spoilt by the family; hugged, kissed, and cuddled by everyone who the parents allowed near their beautiful son.

The whole of the village community is invited into the house to admire the son of Rasheed and Mehetai. One by one they shuffle pass the cot leaving flowers and gifts as a sign of respect and joy for the new-born member of a very tightknit community. After seven days, the local Iman also welcomes Haleem into the Islamic fold and, of course, carries out the religious ceremony, Aqeeqah, which means a shaving of the hair, weighing it and selling it for charitable purposes.

Obviously, growing up in the Indian state of Andhra Pradesh would not be without its problems, seeing as though 91% of the state is in Hindu hands and only a small minority of Muslims occupied the state; roughly 6,5%.

At this moment in time these facts did not matter. However, later, they would play an immense role in the development of Haleem.

After the excitement of Haleem's birth things in Ongole return too normal. A hot, moist summer pursued by monsoon rains that frequent Andhra Pradesh after thrusting southwards from their source in Bangladesh. Haleem's family continue to exist like they have done through generations; a struggle, sometimes happy and sometimes sad like most people do.

In certain parts of India these struggles are more intensive with wretched poverty being rife in and, surrounding the major metropoles, Calcutta, Delhi, Mumbai (Bombay), to name just a few. However, this was not such a problem which Haleem's family had to deal with. Being Muslims in a majority state run by Hindus was their biggest problem, just like their counterparts in Northern India, and Pakistan. Discrimination was part and parcel of their daily lives.

Rasheed was lucky enough to have a good education and worked as a professional, so it was not such a problem. Other, lower-caste Muslims suffered much more. In addition, with the proud birth of their first son, Haleem's parents could walk the streets of their hometown with their heads held high.

"Mehetai darling, do you think it is normal for a one-year-old baby boy to be playing with female dolls that you purchased just in case he was a she, heaven forbid? And rejecting building bricks, Lego, cricket balls and other boys' things?" Rasheed enquired to his innocent wife.

"Oh, silly Rasheed, our Haleem is much too young to know the difference between boys' things and girls! Let him walk properly first and then you will see how our lovely boy will then do the things every proud father expects their son to do!"

Although, still very young Haleem, is attracted to bright colours, including pink, but there was no need to worry as it was quite normal for many young male toddlers to be fascinated by non-macho things. So, without paying too much attention to these early attractions, Haleem's mother thought nothing about it and, Rasheed was much too busy earning money to maintain the families elevated position in the village.

Only when Haleem reaches the age where he toddles around the house and begins to venture out into the surrounding garden did his father begin to doubt about his son's curious rejection of many boy's things. He prefers to play the role of a mini-dancer with his collection of plush animals given as presents throughout his first year of existence.

"Here Haleem come and kick a ball with daddy! OK, if you don't want to do that then we'll go and build castles in the sand pit at the bottom of the garden!" Rasheed attempts to entice Haleem into doing things that boys do after coming home from a very tiring day at the office.

Haleem rushes into the house crying his eyes out and the welcoming arms of his loving mother reach out to comfort him.

"Darling, do not force our Haleem to do these things, when he wants to, he will play such games with you, but please do not expect a one and half year-old toddler to become the famous cricketer like Sachin Tendulkar!" She laughs and calms Rasheed's doubting thoughts about his son.

"Sure, you are right, but I am so proud of my beautiful son I only want the best for him, I hope you understand darling!"

"Of course, but we cannot rush him, he will soon start playing the game's most boys do so do not worry."

After being comforted by his mum, Haleem ceases to cry and decides to go to his bedroom to play with his favourite cuddly toy, a huge, dancing, pink and multi-coloured elephant.

Six months later: Haleem is now a beautiful, but highly-strung toddler who tends to cry quite a lot when being forced by his dad to play games that he believes are suitable for two-year-old boys. In addition, frustrations grow between father and son and, of course, Haleem's loving mother who protects him at any price. Even to the extent of his childhood friends, all girls, is a point of contention between Rasheed and Mehetai.

"He really should be playing with the neighbour's boys and not dancing with the girls, there must be something wrong with Haleem darling!"

"No, no, you have it all wrong, he is an only child and many 'only children' at a very early age, male or female, are attracted to the opposite sex because of their inner desire to have a brother or sister darling, it is normal!"

"Sure, OK, then let us provide Haleem with his inner desire for a sibling and then hopefully he will lose these foolish habits!"

One year later, with Haleem now ready to enter playschool, Mehetai gives birth to their second child, a beautiful girl. Naturally, being Muslim, a female child does not attract the attention of the villagers or the local cleric, but still for Haleem's parents, it is a wonderful experience to have two wonderful healthy children and now their family is complete.

"See darling Rasheed, it will only be a matter of time before Haleem does typical boy's things now he has a tiny sister to protect and your dream of having a real boy will come true!" Mehetai whispers and kisses her husband on the forehead as mother and daughter lay in each other's arms.

"Sure, Haleem will be entering play school soon and I am sure that things will change, and these silly habits of his will become history!" Rasheed smiles and leaves his loving, gentle wife to recover from the painful birth of their second child.

"Haleem, come with me and leave your new-born sister and mother to recover, I'll read you Kipling's Jungle Book before you go to bed, I'm sure you will enjoy that!"

Rasheed takes the hand of his son, who reluctantly leaves the room with a hue tear running down his cheek.

"Haleem, darling, what is it, why are you so upset? Rasheed take the baby and let me give Haleem a huge cuddle before he goes to bed!"

He rushes to the side of the bed gasping for air and with tears running down his cheeks,

"Mummy, mummy, will you still love me as much now you have another baby?"

"Of course, my darling, now run along with daddy, it's time for bed and you must sleep long because tomorrow is your first day at play school, daddy will take you."

"No, no, you must take me not daddy!"

"But I cannot, daddy will make sure you arrive safe and help you find some new friends at school, now be a good boy, I am tired and need to sleep!" She kisses him once again but can hardly control the tears running down his cheeks.

"Now come along Haleem, stop acting like a little girl and come to bed!"

Rasheed drags Haleem out of the room and takes him to his bedroom, removes Jungle Book from the bookshelf hoping to calm his highly-strung son down by reading the wonderful words of Rudyard Kipling, to no avail!

"Enough is enough Haleem, I have attempted to be loving to you and I know you are upset because mummy has a new baby, but tomorrow you will go to playschool, find new friends and your life will become much more interesting. So, if you don't want me to read and do not shut up, I'll leave!"

Haleem turns his back on his daddy, still whimpering and longing for his mummy to comfort him. Rasheed storms out of the bedroom leaving his son to cry himself to sleep!

Will things ever be the same again? We shall see…

Early next morning, and still under protest, Rasheed has no idea how to get Haleem to playschool without Mehetai's help. Feeling very weak she drags herself out of bed, gets dressed, picks her new-born daughter out of the cot and assisted by Rasheed, they go arm in arm to the local playschool.

"Welcome to our wonderful playschool Haleem, I am sure you will have a most enjoyable time here before you start proper school, please run along and join the other children." Haleem stands frozen in front of the headmistress of Ongole's local playschool with his hand clamped into his mother's hand who is also standing carrying Haleem's sister.

"Haleem, please let go and do as the lovely lady says, I will be here later to meet you, don't worry darling you will love it here!"

Haleem stares with his huge, moist, almond shaped eyes, into his mother's eyes as she attempts to release his hand. The headmistress stares down at the behaviour of the child and thinks,

"Nothing unusual about this this, seen it a thousand times before!"

At last, Haleem let's go and is ushered inside the main school room by the headmistress where other children, who had all endured the same initiation process, are rushing around, playing, laughing and, generally doing what most three-year-old children tend to do, enjoying each other's company. Boys in one corner, girls in the other!

Haleem bee-lines towards the girl's corner, ignoring the other boys roughing and tumbling with boy's things; toy cars, trucks, diggers, footballs, toy tools, plastic cricket bats and balls. In fact, everything that tiny male toddlers tend to play with.

He sits, cross legged between two girls who are fascinated by this alien figure who plonks himself down and commences to play with dolls and other girly things on offer!

Normally boys tend to bully the girls and the girls prefer to avoid their male counterparts at this very tender age, but this boy seemed quite different, and within minutes, he was adopted as one of them. All the girls fell immediately in love with this gentle character who preferred their ways instead of the other boys, who generally acted like mini-monkeys, or shy dopes, when confronted with girls.

By this time, Haleem had forgotten his mother and was enjoying every minute of being among the girls, acting, dancing, playing, laughing, giggling, and generally having a great time. The other boys in the group did not notice that one of them was seemingly enjoying the company of girls because at this age, kids do not care about such things, they just want to play and have fun.

The headmistress peers over to the new arrival, smiles and thinks,

"Well, this Haleem is certainly different to the other boys in the group, but never mind, he'll soon contact them and could well be the 'bridge' between the two, now that would be nice!"

The two years spent at the Ongole playschool were heaven for Haleem and the many friends he made, boys and girls, certainly helps him to ease the very strong bond between mother and son. He becomes one of the most popular boys in the group and, not only with his class comrades. The staff just love his gentle way of breaking down barriers between boys and girls. His male friends love his humour and talent, always ready to stand out and act in front of the group by taking on different roles, a born entertainer who everybody loves, even at the tender age between three and six.

Haleem dances, acts, sings and, is always in the main role when the playschool puts on a play or musical for the parents. The other children just look on in awe as this mini-talent wows the audiences. Parents and staff applause after Haleem with, his group of actors and dancers, strut their stuff. In addition, when asked to appear at the local theatre, the school agrees and, naturally, Haleem plays the leading role in a musical comedy that has the whole village laughing and praising the very young talents performing in front of them, especially Haleem.

Rasheed, Haleem's father, now begins to realise why his only son is slightly different from the rest of the boys in the village as he looks on and admires how at this tender toddler age, he manages to mesmerise the crowd with subtle movements, smiles, perfect timing, and pleasure, that he obviously loves whilst performing.

"So, therefore I failed to understand why Haleem is so different from other boys, he is destined to become an actor, entertainer, or something like that when he grows up. However, I do hope when he is older, he chooses a sensible profession, but for now I am so proud of our tiny son!" Rasheed confesses to his on-looking and, very proud wife and mother of Haleem.

"Yes darling, you do not have to fear about Haleem, he will succeed in the world he is destined to conquer and that is why maybe sometimes he acts quite peculiar compared to other lads of his age, sure!" Mothers tend to have a 'sixth sense' about such things and maybe she was right just like most women are.

Haleem leaves his local playschool and enters junior school where the serious side of life begins for all children in India, preparing for the future. Depending on what cast children come from, the expectancy levels placed upon children are always different. However, the main object for parents is to give their children the possibility to improve on their status meaning; at the lowest level finances dictate how much a child can achieve. These children have the most difficult task in achieving a higher status. Those above find it easier, but only through hard work, hours of study and exam results. India is a huge country with diverse ethnic backgrounds, plus huge differences between privileged and under-privileged children.

Hence, the pressure put upon children is immense, like Japan and other Far East countries, especially those children from middle and higher casts. Education is the gateway to the world and, children from middle and higher castes are destined to improve the status of their families by achieving successful exam results through further studies that elevate their children and give the family pride and respect.

However, children who are not so fortunate from lower-caste families living in the vast countryside, agricultural areas or, those who inhabit slums surrounding major cities, have normally no chance to improve the status of their families. Albeit, a tiny minority have achieved some form of success, but these are rare diamonds among millions!

The first steps on this long and arduous path commence in junior schools and, depending on which school children attend and the financial status of their parents, determines how much Indian children can achieve. Finance dictates and it is obvious that in such a diverse country as India, where the huge divide between rich and poor will never be bridged, those who have the most, generally achieve the most. However, there are exceptions to the rule with many examples of people who escape the system through extreme talent, dedication, and damn hard work; maybe a Slum Dog Millionaire or two?

Haleem is lucky, his parents do not belong to the millions of impoverished people sentenced to life in huge slums or living off the land, dictated by rich landowners surrounding country villages. Rasheed, and Mehetai, come from lower-middle backgrounds, were quite well educated and, could offer Haleem a reasonably solid start to life in a respected junior school simply because they could pay the fees, books and other costs required at this level.

Junior School and further recognition of Haleem's precocious talent

Haleem enters Ongole Junior High School proudly wearing his finely pressed uniform, including a green-striped blazer with the school badge embroidered onto his left lapel. A proud sign that children wearing the blazer could afford the school, and others less fortunate, attended a different department of the school without affluent blazers.

Along with other boys of his age (From junior school onwards boys and girls are separated), he proudly enters the classroom with his satchel strapped across his back, reserved only for those children whose parents could afford the fees, an elite class in other words.

After studying reports passed on by the local playschool, a stern looking female teacher looks into Haleem' s huge brown, warm eyes and says,

"Ha, ha, we have an entertainer among us, nice, but my boy, forget your entertaining, you are here to learn the basics, mathematics, geography, science and other important subjects! Entertaining you can do after school if you have time because from now on every evening will be spent doing homework and your parents expect you to achieve, so forget your life as an entertainer for the time being, there's real work to be done!"

Haleem bows his head shyly refusing to eyeball the teacher realizing that this period in his life is going to be tough, but he must please his parents and family because they are supporting and financing his life. So, he silently vows deep down,

"I hate you, the school and education, but I will buckle down and study just like my parents wish me to because to achieve my goals I must be educated!"

Haleem is quite a clever seven-year-old.

To oppress talent is to lose, but nobody told the school, its teachers and financers. Their only goal was to maintain very high standards of education so junior high school kids can pass on to the very best secondary school. A system implemented basically by the English whilst ruling this wonderful country under The Raj and, adopted by Indians as a sign of their willingness to adhere to western standards.

A very talented and sensitive childlike Haleem would find it utmost difficult maintaining dedication and concentration for his basic studies. However, as in most successful people, a personal drive and determination kicks in in such mundane times helping to tame the 'creative beast from within'. A question of self-discipline and a constant, internal battle, especially through childhood years.

"Haleem my son, how was school today?" Rasheed asks after coming home from a hard day's work at the office.

"Fine, dad, sure, I am doing my best to show you and mum that I will fulfill your trust in me," Haleem answers.

"OK my son, continue with your homework, I see you have much to do, and I do not wish to disturb you."

Rasheed leaves Haleem's bedroom and after three solid hours of revising for a mathematic, history, and geography test, he decides enough is enough and turns on the local radio hoping to find some music or a radio play to listen to, making sure his parents cannot hear anything. He plugs his earphones into the radio. After twiddling the dial for a few minutes, suddenly, the crackly sound of Indian traditional Kuchipudi dance music enters his ears. Then, his soul and heart drifts down to the lower part of his body where his legs start moving to the wonderful music.

Mesmerized by the sounds coming out of his transistor radio given to him by his granddad after achieving entrance to the very best junior high school in the area, Haleem lifts himself out of the chair, grabs the radio and commences, barefoot, to glide across the dusty floor moving gracefully to the music.

"Sure, this is heaven," he thinks.

Minute after minute he moves to the traditional rhythms and, looking at himself in the cracked mirror standing in the corner of his tiny bedroom, he believes he is pretty good and smiles at himself proudly.

"Damn radio keeps cracking up, I must find myself a better way to listen to this quite wonderful music. Maybe if I pass my first year's exam granddad will buy me a tiny television, but first I must complete my homework, be a good boy and hope?"

He sits down behind his books once again, and in a determined mood, studies until he falls asleep at his rather wobbly, wooden, ancient desk.

"Darling Haleem, my boy you are so wonderful!" Mehetai enters the bedroom and gives Haleem a huge kiss on his drooped head that hangs over an open geography book; he's fast asleep. She wakes him up, helps him clean his teeth and then tucks him into bed with a huge goodnight kiss for comfort.

"Dear Haleem, you are so dedicated to your studies, and we are so proud of you!" She whispers in his ear not knowing the true motivation behind hours and hours of study.

"Sleep now darling it is 22.30 PM and you must be up at 06.30 because the school bus waits for nobody." However, before she could finish her sentence Haleem was in a deep sleep dreaming of amazing dancers, music, colorful robes, and certainly not geography books!

During the first year, all male pupils must participate in sporting activities, mainly cricket, which is second only to religion in India, and every boy in Haleem's class always looks forward to the allocated three hours of sport in the curriculum; Haleem hates it!

"Now come on Haleem, show a bit of aptitude, grab the cricket bat and show the rest you are a real man!" Haleem's macho sports teacher mocks him in front of the other pupils after noticing his tendency to prefer dancing on his own alone during sports time. He would often drift off into a dream world whilst warming up for a game of cricket or hockey and, suddenly burst into a song with his legs following. His actions become a point of contention with the sports teacher and after screaming in his ear to come back to reality, Haleem, would normally obey hoping not to offend or awaken any suspicions about his secret desire to dance, and certainly not play cricket or hockey!

Naturally, other boys notice that Haleem has slightly different interests to themselves, and he is now an easy target for their insults especially the bullies in his class start to make fun and torment him.

It is 16.00 PM outside the school gates as a group of bullies decide to wait for Haleem to exit the gate.

"Hey Haleem, you are quite a sissy for a Muslim, or are you a little girl in disguise?" One bully called, Kalem Singh, the ringleader, shouts threateningly as Haleem approaches the outside gates.

"Kalem, you are a bully and have a big mouth, I feel sorry for you!"

"You feel sorry for me, Muslim Pussy; you should feel sorry for yourself because me and the boys are going to give you a lesson in being a real boy instead of prancing around during sports hour like a ballerina!"

One of the other boys grabs Haleem's satchel from behind and tugs him to the ground. The others jump on him and hold him down while Kalem pulls down his trousers!

"Oh, look boys, he really is a boy!"

The others laugh.

"Maybe if I give him a kick in the balls he might change and start acting like a real boy should!"

"Do it, do it, do it!" The others scream and, just before Kalem's boot lands in Haleem's crutch, the art teacher's hand grabs him by the scruff of the neck and yells,

"You, Kalem, are the local bully, and your gang here just love picking on the weakest, now you have bitten off more than you can chew!"

"I am not weak," Haleem squeals, "just let me get Kalem alone and I will show him who and what a real boy is!"

"OK, enough is enough, no more fighting here, you Kalem and the others will report to the headmaster tomorrow and you Haleem will report to my office tomorrow too, OK! Now make sure you all go home, no more bullying otherwise I will deal with you all personally and your parents will know too!"

Kalem turns away with the others and sneers, "pussy!" They all laugh at his foul mouth, luckily, he is far enough away so the art teacher cannot not hear yet another insult.

"Haleem are you OK dear boy?"

"Yes sir, it's nothing please let me get the bus now and we can talk tomorrow."

"If anything happens again just let me know and I'll deal with them, Oh, and by the way, I have noticed that you have a certain interest in the arts, dancing, and other cultural things, maybe I can help you sometime."

"Thank you, sir, yes you are right, I just love to dance and listen constantly to Kuchipudi and other classical Indian music after I have finished my homework and it would be quite wonderful to speak to you about it because nobody else here seems to know anything about this fantastic tradition!"

"We shall chat tomorrow, Haleem, now be safe!"

"Please do not worry sir, I can look after myself you know, sure!" They both smile as Haleem picks up his satchel and rushes to the bus.

"Darling, what happened?" Haleem's mother, in a panic, greets her bruised, grazed and dusty son as he enters the door.

"Nothing mum, nothing at all and don't worry everything is OK I just had a fall that's all!" He answers.

"Look at you, something more serious must have happened! Was it those ghastly bullies led by that wretch Kalem?"

"No mum, I am alright. Someone nice helped me after my fall, everything is just fine!"

He trots off to his bedroom, opens his books and proceeds to complete his homework before listening once again to his crackly radio hoping to tune into the wonderful, Kuchipudi music, and most of all, dance to it.

"Rasheed darling, I'm sure Haleem has been in a fight at school, he came home looking like a battered stray dog (common in India)." Mehetai tells her husband.

"Where is he now?"

"In his room doing his homework, I'm sure it was those bullies led by that awful Kalem who did it, but Haleem refuses to tell me!"

Rasheed knocks on the bedroom door,

"Haleem dear boy what happened?"

"Nothing dad, I just fell, and the kind art teacher picked me up and helped me, it was nothing at all, please tell mum not to worry, I can look after myself!" Haleem defiantly answers.

"OK, I believe you, but if anything does happen or you are bullied, please let me know because it is obvious your life is planned for much greater things than the jealous bullies at school and we do not want anything to deter you from that!"

"Sure dad, I understand and please do not fuss about nothing, now let me please finish my homework I have much to do!"

"OK, we will be eating soon, so do as much as you can, exams are coming up and you must pass!"

The next day Haleem does as he is ordered and visits the art teacher during the morning break, his name, Shiva Kumar. He knocks on the door.

"Haleem please enter and close the door after you." He enters.

"Now tell me Haleem what do you know about Indian traditional dancing? Maybe I can help you because I am fascinated by this wonderful tradition too. I have many books and literature and, if you wish, I can lend them to you, so you can study them."

"Please sir, that would be wonderful, but please do not divulge my secret to anybody. After homework in the evenings, I put on my transistor radio and tune in to the musical stations hoping that they play some Kuchipudi music and then I dance along, it is wonderful sir, just wonderful!"

"Haleem, I understand you and will help you during your stay here in any way I can; it will remain a secret between us and by the way, I have read your playschool report, noticed you are quite a good actor and entertainer; would you like to come along to auditions for my school play based upon one of Dicken's great works, Oliver Twist. I am converting it into a junior version and need some more actors from your age group, but not many of the boys are interested so I am asking the girls department to fill in the male roles and they just love the idea!"

"Oh sir, that would be tremendous, but what about my homework?"

"Do not worry we can rehearse during sports hours. I will arrange with the headmaster that I need you for the school play, very prestigious indeed I'll arrange everything with the girl's school, I'm sure you will love it!"

"No doubt sir, can I play Oliver, sure?"

"We shall see, but according to your reports from playschool you could well land the part! So, run along now and here are one or two books relating to Kuchipudi dancing, its history, traditions and culture, I am sure they will interest you. In addition, I will inform you about rehearsals for the play!"

For the first time since Haleem has attended this dreadful school, he feels happy inside and, silently thanks the bullies for being what they are, just bullies, because without them the art teacher would not have saved him; he believes.

After a year's study, Haleem, manages to scrape through his first exams to slip through to the second year. It was mental torture, but with pure dedication, determination, and the help of his decrepit, ageing transistor radio, he succeeds. The family visits and congratulate Haleem for his academic prowess. His granddad, after hearing from Haleem's mother that his one desire is a TV in his room, brings along a Jurassic black box that resembles a TV.

Haleem smiles and is over the moon after receiving this wonderful gift.

"You deserve it my boy, we are so proud of you and your achievements at school. We have even heard you are about to play in Dicken's, Oliver Twist, in a school play to celebrate the end of your first year at the school!"

"Yes granddad, you are all invited and, Sir Shiva Kumar, our art teacher, gave me this marvelous opportunity to play the leading role; I am so happy!"

The rest of the family clap their hands as Haleem leaves the room to finish off his homework for the evening; he feels like a star (Maybe he has a premonition?)!

After passing through a most difficult first year at Junior High Haleem enters his second year, and with the constant support and recognition of his undoubted talents, his art teacher, Shiva Kumar, offers to give him acting and classical dancing lessons after school hours. This offer Haleem just cannot refuse and after asking permission from his parents, he can now participate with several other very talented children, musicians, poets, actors, and authors, who are always greeted with suspicion from fellow pupils because of their outstanding, precocious talents.

Misconceptions from other students often lead to bullying, discrimination, and dislike, especially when male pupils possess such artistic talents; girls normally have an easier ride.

However, after appearing in several classical Indian, and English school plays and musicals, fellow male pupils gradually rid themselves of such prejudices and, begin to respect enjoy the talents of their colleagues. After all, not everybody can become a super Indian cricket star; the dream of most young male pupils!

Haleem was no exception and, in his second-year life becomes easier because even boys wish to 'hang out' with him; and girls adore him, which made him feel quite embarrassed. But he feels mostly at ease with girls whose only desire was to pamper and spoil him.

"Haleem fancy a game of cricket after school, we are meeting over at the derelict factory, and you can spin a few overs if you wish?" Haleem's best friend, Kalyan, inquires.

"Why not? I would love to join in if the other boys don't start to tease and that wretched bully Kalem is not involved!"

"Don't worry about him Haleem, if he starts bullying and teasing, I'll take care of him!"

Haleem goes home with Kalyan, and they change clothes ready for a game of cricket with the other lads. At school, Haleem is quite a handy spin bowler, which requires a special talent of twisting the cricket ball in midair whilst mesmerizing the batsman. There is no brute force or strength required. Just a subtle amount of elegance whilst tossing the ball towards the opponent. The school asked Haleem to join the school cricket team, he declined because of his other artistic obligations, but a game with the boys seemed like a pleasant thing to do and a couple of hours in the fresh air was also welcoming.

They enter the dusty, wind-blown arena situated among surrounding, derelict buildings. Other boys are busy forming teams for the evening's game. Everybody gets picked except for Haleem as he stands alone and is last to be chosen. Kalem, the bully and captain of one of the teams, refuses to take Haleem. So, Kalyan tugs him over to his team to stop further embarrassment. Haleem feels anger growing inside and a determination to succeed against all odds.

His teammates start to grumble, but Kalyan has none of it. The game commences with the other team bowling first. The best batsmen start proceedings against furious fast bowlers from Kalem's team. They manage to knock up a reasonable score and after they are bowled out, the weaker batsmen take their place between the wickets made up of anything that can stand vertical, mainly a block of bricks!

The weakest batsmen are normally skittled out with ease because their talents are bowling. So, Haleem enters as final batsman as Kalem grabs the rock-hard cricket ball and screams,

"Haleem, you pussy, I am going to blow you away with one fowl swoop, be careful and duck because this ball might damage your delicate, manicured fingernails!"

The other boys laugh as a screamer of a ball flies past Haleem's left ear. He drops the bat on to the wicket and it crumbles!

"Howzat!" Screams Kalem and doubles over in laughter as his teammates run over to congratulate him!

Haleem attempts to run out of the ground, but Kalyan grabs his arm and say's,

"Are you going to chicken out to this bully and prove to everybody you really are a Pussy? Or are you going to stay and fight for your growing reputation among the boys and prove to him you are one of us? I trust you Haleem, so do not runaway like a spoilt cissy!"

Haleem eyeballs Kalyan with a pair of moist, nearly tearful eyes and vows,

"OK, but only for you my dear friend will I stay and not be a coward, sure!"

Kalyan's side commence to bowl and things are reasonably even with neither side gaining a real advantage until Kalem takes over the batting and slams nearly every ball delivered all over the ground. Not one bowler can get a ball pass him so Kalyan whispers into Haleem's ear,

"Your turn!"

He tosses the ball to him and, a tentative Haleem enters the arena face to face with his worst enemy, Kalem the bully!

He walks to the opposite side of the wicket and prepares to bowl the first ball from his first over consisting of six balls. He accurately measures out his run as the opposing team commence to laugh, whistle and boo!

"The Pussy is about to get slammed to hell," they yell and Kalem cannot believe his luck as he gets ready to slam any ball delivered by, Haleem the Sissy, out of the arena and out of sight!

Haleem gently runs up and delivers his first ball! It spins in the air and hits the dusty ground with a gentle 'plonk'! Kalem approaches it and, with a huge 'whack' sends it skywards towards the outer boundary marked by empty tin cans and bricks.

"SIX," the umpire yells! Kalyan cringes, and his teammates nearly start a riot!

"How could you let this soft sissy bowl against the beast Kalem, you Wally?!"

"Quiet you, be silent, it's not over yet, give him at least a chance to find his rhythm," Kalyan warns.

The fielder tosses the battered ball to Haleem once again, who is slightly shaken and red-faced by the ferocious attack on his first ball, but inside he feels he can do much better.

This time he takes a slightly longer run and twists the ball before it leaves his hand. It flies gently towards Kalem, who foolishly and, quite arrogantly, steps out of his crease to thrash the thing into oblivion!

The ball starts to tumble, then spin, and just as Kalem's bat is about to launch it into outer space, it shimmies out of reach and flashes past the bat narrowly missing the wicket by a hair's breadth!

"Beginners luck you Pussy, next time I'll ram the ball down your throat!"

Haleem ignores the threat, catches the ball and goes for his third ball feeling slightly more confident! Kalem returns to his wicket convinced the last ball was just a fluke and vows to hammer the ball right back to where it came from!

The other boys in Kalem's team are now silent, no more yowling or insults. Kalyan's teammates are also mesmerized by the whole scenario as Haleem makes his approach. The ball leaves his left hand (most talented people are left-handed, the writer of this fantastic novel too!), it drops shorter, in fact, "just right," thinks Kalem, as he thunders forward determined to slam the ball back down Haleem's throat as he promised earlier!

It thumps on the ground and, with his attention focused totally on the movement of the ball, Kalem takes a huge swing! Just a vital split second is required between bat and ball for a perfect hit or miss! The ball bounces into the air!

"Perfect," Kalem thinks, and just as he thrusts his bat forward, sure he was about to smack it down the throat of the Sissy opposing him; it swirls to the left just kissing the side of the bat, and wickedly spins to the right again! The thrust of the bat gives it even more spin and it hurtles, out of control centrally, towards the wicket!

"Howzat!!!" Kalyan's teammates scream and rush over to Haleem, grab him and toss him in the air! He feels like a Lord's (Famous Cricket Ground in London) Magician as he is tossed up and down by his teammates!

Kalem snarls, "It was a fluke softy, just a fluke!"

Kalem's teammates boo him off the park and all rush over to congratulate Haleem on that magical spin-ball! A wonderful thing in the hearts of all fanatic cricket fans in India and, Haleem the 'Pussy', had delivered a moment of pure magic!

"Kalyan, dear friend, thank you for this opportunity to participate in this marvelous game, I am most honored, but now it is time to go home, I must do my homework, see you tomorrow!"

"Please Haleem, rethink your decision and come and play in the school team!"

"No dear friend, my ambitions lye somewhere else and I must concentrate fully on my goals, not wickets, thank you anyway!"

He wanders off six-foot taller than before, and very proud. However, luring behind a huge banyan tree Haleem is not aware that the school bully was waiting for him. He passes the tree as Kalem jumps out in front of him and grabs his neck! Haleem stands with his fists ready to fight to the death as Kalem, in a friendly voice says,

"Haleem, my dear friend! That was a wonderful ball you bowled me out with and certainly not a fluke! I am sorry for constantly bullying you and promise never to do it again!" A snarl turns into a grin as he pats Haleem gently on his shoulder!

Haleem shaking violently, smiles back at Kalem, promises to forgive him for the bullying and hopes they become friends! They shake hands, smile and laugh.

"See you tomorrow at school Haleem and please promise to teach me how to bowl like that, fantastic!" Kalem says.

"I promise Kalem, see you tomorrow!"

Haleem heads home feeling wonderful. He sings to himself, looks up in the sky thanking Allah for this wonderful moment in his very young life.

Minutes later he enters the family abode smiling from cheek to cheek.

"Haleem, you are looking very proud of yourself, what happened, I thought you was playing cricket a game you normally avoid?"

"Yes father, and guess what happened, I bowled Kalem the school bully out with a wicked spin ball from another planet! First, he was very angry, but then he jumped out from a hiding place and congratulated me for the brilliant ball! We are now friends' dad, and he has promised never to bully me again, wonderful!"

"Son, I am so proud of you, and will you be taking up that offer to play in the school cricket team? A great honor for me and the family?"

"No sir, I have no time because of after school activities with Sir Shiva, my arts mentor, they take up too much time and that is more important than a silly cricket game!"

Haleem's dad smiles, but deep down inside he feels upset. However, his son's happiness is more important and nothing else really matters; to quote a famous metal evergreen!

"Dad, I will go to my room to study, we are rapidly approaching the end of the school year and I must pass my exams!"

"Good boy Haleem, that's the spirit, but please keep that confounded music on the TV turned down and, not too late in bed!"

"Sure," Haleem answers.

After this very positive moment in his life, Haleem, now very confident, and enjoying the respect of his fellow pupils, breezes through the final year at Junior High. As a grand finale for the leaving pupils, Sir Shiva Kumar, arranges a musical that everybody around the globe adores; Kipling's, Jungle Book, and guess who he chooses to play the leading role, Mowgli?

Yes, you are all right, Haleem!

Weeks of preparation pass proving to be very intensive for all concerned, especially those revising and studying for their eleven plus exams implemented in all respectable Indian schools by the English Raj.

However, nothing will deter Haleem from being a perfect Mowgli. He works so hard at school, then in the evening rehearses. Slowly, signs of physical and mental exhaustion begin to appear.

"Dear Haleem, please take it easy child, you will have a burn-out soon if you do not slow down," Shiva Kumar advises.

"Sir, I must achieve the best exam results possible and my grand desire to play this fantastic role for the school as well! I will not give up until I have achieved both!"

Sir Shiva smiles and thinks,

"Boy, this child is so talented, determined and ambitious, how can I stop him?"

"OK, final dress rehearsals are the day after tomorrow, your final exams next week. So, you have the whole weekend to rest and promise me you will!" A stern Sir Shiva stares into Haleem's rather dark-rimmed eyes.

"OK Sir, I promise! But first rehearsal, I am so excited!"

The grand day arrives, and Haleem boasts a huge smile after hearing he scraped through his eleven plus and now can go to a suitable secondary Technical School, not grammar school, not quite. He enters the school theatre and makes his way to backstage ready for make-up feeling very excited indeed.

"Haleem, my dear boy, congratulations on your exams and now you can pursue your dreams even further!" Sir Shiva smiles and hugs his prodigy!

"Now boy, go out there and wow your audience because you are the main player everybody cannot wait to see!"

"I will sir, I will!"

The curtains rise, the music begins, enter Balou the bear played by Haleem's dear friend, Kalyan. Spectators sit with mesmerized expectancy as they hear the whistling of a young boy merrily wandering through the jungle surrounding his village. Haleem enters, the crowd gasp as Balou and Mowgli meet for the first time and, the rest is history; even in this version acted out at Junior High School in Ongole!

After the final curtain falls, spectators, parents, teachers, and fellow pupils, stand and applause the actors and actresses starring in this wonderful musical played out in front of their eyes. Haleem leads them out to rapturous applause and bows. A tingling rush of adrenalin flows through his body, enters his buzzing brain and, he now knows this is his destiny, sure!

They bow and bow again as a very proud, Sir Shiva Kumar, enters the stage and approaches Haleem. He holds up his arm and they bow together! The spectators raise the roof once again as every single player hug and kisses each other; a majestic, unforgettable moment of pure ecstasy for Haleem and his colleagues.

However, only a very few will go on to achieve even further popularity; they do not know yet who? But Haleem has a rough idea!

Dark years of confusion

For any budding, prodigious talent, the inevitable must appear in the form of a dark period in everybody's lives called puberty; Haleem is no exception. After entering a respectable, Technical Boarding School in Hyderabad, the main town of Andhra Pradesh and, entering his teens. Haleem, like any other child, becomes slightly worried at the prospect of venturing through a peculiar time where the mind and body tend to explode.

Puberty, for most children is difficult. However, for many highly strung, sensitive, and extremely talented children, life can become hell.

Without wishing to speak to his parents about these strange happenings, Haleem embroils himself even further in his ambitions to become something quite extraordinary.

His long days become unbearable at school, studying, missing his mum and dad and generally feeling quite uncomfortable in his raging body! He also spends many hours in the dormitory alone, dancing, singing, copying classical Indian dancers, and studying images depicted in books he borrows from the school library.

His real passion now is listening to the classical sounds of Ravi Shankar during breaks and moving to the wonderful, ingenious sounds pouring out of his sitar. At the weekends, after travelling home, Haleem's parents do not mind the noise exiting his bedroom behind a closed door because they also love Ravi Shankar. Hoping one day their son will one day become as famous as this glorious representative of all things good in Indian tradition and culture. However, they are mistaken by Haleem's passion for Indian classical sitar music because they are not observing him moving elegantly across the floor of his bedroom resembling a certain, Billy Elliot, whose only desire was to become a famous English ballet dancer.

Haleem practices until 22.00 PM and then collapses into his bed dreaming of the future entertaining thousands just like Billy Elliot or Rudolf Nureyev did; in a slightly different traditional manner of course.

They become a massive influence in his life parallel to studying the intricate movements and listening to Indian classical dancing. He develops a love for ballet where the combination of elegance and beauty is driving him to seek something similar within Indian classical dances.

Early one Sunday morning, roughly 03.00 AM, he wakes up, perspiring with excitement after being woke up by a recurrent dream; floating images of himself dressed like, and dancing with, a group of Indian traditional dancers. He remembers the literature given to him by his early mentor, Sire Shiva Kumar, at junior school which he had pushed to the back of his bookshelf filled with mathematic, biological, historical, geographical, and other school literature. Mundane learning books necessary to succeed at school.

"Now where are those gems that Sir Shiva Kumar gave me? I need to study Kuchipudi, it is my destiny of that, I am sure!" Haleem convinces himself.

He puts on his table lamp holding a cheap, dusty, cob-webbed ancient Osram 12-volt bulb. It flickers in the darkness surrounded by nocturnal, annoying moths and flying bugs searching for some ragged cloth to feed on or blood to suck. Luckily, in the dormitory, spiders were quite abundant ready to devour them.

"Damn moths get out of my way, aha, here they are!"

Over in the corner and smothered in dust he detects them!

"Yes, here they are! Kuchipudi my destiny, yes!"

He dusts the books down and places them under his pillow knowing deep down inside they will assist him in his goal to become a famous dancer and actor when he grows up. But first he must combat the dreaded puberty years and that is something not many children seem capable of dealing with sensibly!

Being aware that a very talented boy was attending their recommended Boarding School, the expectancy levels among the art department are very high. All the necessary documentation, videos, and other moments of glory had been forwarded by Haleem's art teacher from Junior School. After evaluation by the board of teachers, they agree to nurture even further the natural talents that Haleem possesses.

Parallel to his special, allocated status and maintaining the emphasis on his basic, curriculum studies, the board of directors decide to designate him to a highly skillful, talented teacher, who predominantly gives extra music, acting, and dancing lessons to boys possessing outstanding talents, his name, Mr. Radeem Singh Esq.

Mr. Singh, apart from being a teacher, is also well known in the entertainment, theatre world in Hyderabad and if theatres require child actors or performers, he would oblige with boys from the school. This cooperative work helped enhance the prestigious reputation of the school in the area.

Haleem rapidly adapts to his new surroundings and wins the admiration and respect of most teachers, apart from PE teachers, who look upon Haleem as being rather a 'softy' apart from his superb, elegant spin-bowling cricket skills.

Compared to other pupils raging towards puberty with exploding bursts of acne smothering their faces and, exaggerated showing off in front of female pupils from the girl's school across the street, he finds it rather difficult to make contact, apart from those who also participate in after school music, acting and dance lessons. In fact, the other boys who sleep in a huge dormitory with Haleem tend to behave rather chauvinistic and act macho towards their 'softer' colleagues. This causes obvious friction, which appears in the form of gentle bullying, teasing and other things that young, budding, male teenagers tend to do.

Haleem, of course, is used to bullying at Junior School. However, with nobody to protect him at this school, things were about to become difficult.

Boys will be boys and noticeably the rougher, tougher kids, at this tender age, tend to rule the roost, especially in Boarding Schools. After a few minor incidents; bugs being put in his bed, harassment in the showers after sport with other boys pouring bottles of stinging shampoo over his head and turning him into a sea of bubbles; spiking his meals with insects, tarring his underpants with boot polish plus other quite nasty things, Haleem decides it is time for action!

Not wishing too tell-tale on his roommates because that would only make things worse, he decides to enter martial arts classes on offer at school. Initially, when the other boys hear of his intention, they tease him even further, which ultimately reaches the ears of Mr. Singh. So, he orders Haleem for a chat in his office and demands that Haleem tells him the truth about the other boy's unacceptable behavior. He refuses, but promises not to neglect the extra artistic lessons given by Mr. Singh and tells him,

"Sir, please do not worry about me, I will soon be able to look after myself, and I am determined to succeed here!"

"OK Haleem, but if things escalate even further, I order you to tell me about it!"

"Sure!" was his reply.

Haleem joins a group of martial art pupils and to his surprise many of them are skinny, rather weak examples of teenage youths like himself. There is only one of the larger boys among them, quite porky in fact. A quiet, shy boy, who shares Haleem's dormitory and obviously endures bullying and teasing from the other boys too, his name; Dileep.

"Hi Dileep, what are you doing here?" Haleem friendly inquires.

"None of your business and keep yourself to yourself, I do not need any sympathy from a 'pussy' like you!"

"OK Dileep, I was only being friendly and if you change your mind, I would like to be your friend."

Dileep grunts and enters the gymnasium with the others.

Haleem, being the first time in the group, is introduced by their black-belt judo teacher, Mr. Sadeem.

"Boys, we have a new pupil, Haleem, please greet him because I am sure he is suffering just like many of you have suffered at the hands of our bullies, but that is all about to change for him, and you all know why!"

The boys laugh and cheer before Mr. Sadeem commences with the first lessons. He takes Haleem aside and assigns Dileep to help him through his initiation ceremony, Dileep grunts again. Haleem smiles, as Dileep silently, but swiftly, grabs him by the collar of his PT shirt and thumps him on the ground with a huge smile!

Haleem, shaken, but not stirred, arises, laughs, and says,

"Dileep, that was pretty good, now show me how to do it!"

They both smile, Mr. Sadeem too, as the ice breaks between the two and they continue their lesson.

After hearing that Dileep and Haleem are now taking judo, karate, and other martial arts lessons, the other boys in the dormitory tend to keep a healthy distance away from the unlikely duo who rapidly become great friends.

Haleem, the multi-talented, artistic orientated teenager, and his huge, shy friend, Dileep, seem made for each other.

"Dileep, why are you so shy with the other boys, and why do you not join them in their naughty escapades is it because you are a Muslim too?" Haleem asks.

"Haleem, please do not ask, but I can tell you one thing, my dad used to beat me because I was quiet, rather fat and not so intelligent as he demanded. That is why I landed here in a Hindu majority Boarding School instead of a Muslim Grammar School to try and make a real Muslim man of me. He said I bring shame among the family, and he hates me!"

"Don't worry Dileep, we are now friends, I like you very much and we will prove to the world that we losers can also be winners!"

Dileep smiles as a huge tear runs down his chubby, spotty cheek.

"Haleem, you are the first real friend I have ever had, and I will do all I can to help you with your ambition to become a famous actor and dancer, I promise!"

From this day on the two of them become inseparable. They both exceed in their martial arts classes achieving junior blue belts within two years in judo and karate. Dileep attends Haleem's dancing and acting lessons when he can, and they both help each other with their homework.

The other boys become suspicious of this peculiar friendship and decide to give the pair a harsh lesson in 'true manliness', but being cowards, they do not trust themselves to hurt either one of them just in case revenge might be vicious.

So, from a distance they decide to commence with verbal warfare against Haleem and Dileep.

The usual insults are launched at the pair, pussies, softies, homo's, big girls' blouses, etc. However, this does not bother the duo at all because apart from learning different forms of physical self-defense, Mr. Sadeem, also teaches the boys mental strength, a vital part of martial art training.

The first and second years fly by without too much fuss; Haleem and Dileep pass their exams not with ease, but just scrape through. Haleem obviously exceeds with his artistic lessons and appears at several theatres in operas and comedy shows in child roles bringing pride and prestige to the school as they hoped when they first realized what a special talent they had in their midst. Dileep follows Haleem when he can and is totally mesmerized by his friend's display of multi-talents on the theatre stages. Any role that he plays, Haleem seems to master without problems. This does not go unnoticed by agents visiting local theatres searching for fresh, young talents.

One evening after a successful comedy show, Dileep waits backstage for his dear friend. He greets him, and they walk together through the local park back to the school chatting and laughing.

It is 21.00PM as the boys walk through the park innocently, jovially discussing the show as darkness slowly approaches. It is not quite dark yet, but the shadows grow longer as a warm, moist wind blows through the trees, rustling leaves, and disturbing rubbish thrown to the side by park visitors throughout the day, it's an Indian thing, they do not believe in rubbish bins!

The happy pair head towards the exit of the park with school just 500 yards away. Suddenly, out of the shadows four masked figures jump out in front of them armed with cricket bats.

"Hey, you, Muslim, gay softies, did you have a nice time at the theatre because now your happy days are about to end, pray to Allah before we smash your brains to pulp!"

"Dear chap, we are Muslim yes and we are very good friends, but certainly not gay as you ignoramuses tend to believe! In addition, we are blue belt holders in karate and judo, so you have been warned!"

Ignoring Haleem's warning, the leader of the gang screams,

"Fuck all Muslims and gays we hate them!"

One of the gang leaps forward and aims a bat at Dileep's head, he ducks and kicks the assailant in the midriff. He misses his target and falls to the ground. The second one then leaps forward and slams his bat over Dileep's head smashing him to the ground as he attempts to stand up!

Haleem leaps forward as the attacker turns his attention to him attempting to whack his bat over Haleem's head! With one swift movement, he leaps high and launches a foot attack to the assailant's hooded head and kicks with impunity, a perfect hit!

The third Muslim/gay Basher attempts to slam his weapon on Dileep's bleeding head again. Luckily, Haleem sees the attack coming towards his wounded pal, jumps in front of him and receives a whack from the bat across his head too, which knocks him over. He lands on top of Dileep, and the other two, now recovered, proceed to kick, and hit the pair with violent attacks.

Haleem and Dileep attempt to thwart the blows with their arms and hands, but to no avail. Four armed thugs against two unarmed, spirited fighters, no chance!

Running towards the battle, a passerby, after hearing the commotion and screams yells,

"Hey, what the hell is going on there?" He approaches the bloody scene.

"Haleem, Dileep, is that you?"

Haleem recognizes the voice of Mr. Sadeem and screams,

"Help us Sir!"

The attackers realize that a very dangerous savior is approaching. They grab their bats and run into the bushes hoping that Mr. Sadeem does not follow. Luckily, for them, he stays and attends to the boys realizing that both have received heavy wounds from the attacks with blood pouring out their heads.

"Don't worry boys, an ambulance is on its way, I have just telephoned with emergency services, and they will be here as soon as possible!"

He presses a handkerchief on to Haleem's wound attempting to stop the bleeding.

"Sir, please help Dileep, he is unconscious and breathing strangely!"

Mr. Sadeem turns his attention to Dileep who is struggling to breath. He rapidly turns him on his side and pulls his tongue out of his throat!"

Saved by the bell!

"Everything will be alright Haleem, Dileep is OK now, and listen, here comes the ambulance!"

"Thank you, sir." He then passes out.

The ambulance rushes into the park with alarm bells ringing and blue lights flashing. Three medicals rush out to inspect the damage to the boys fully packed with oxygen backpacks and other necessary equipment.

"Sir, please attend to this boy first. He took a heavy crack on the head, and I had to pull his tongue out of his throat, he needs oxygen rapidly I believe," Mr. Sadeem informs the medicals.

Haleem lies unconscious on the ground bleeding from a head wound caused by the cricket bat as another medic rushes over, lifts his eyelids, checks the breathing, and gently lays him on his side as a precautionary measure.

Within minutes both victims are lifted into the ambulance, luckily, both breathing steadily, but unconscious.

"Sir, would you come with us as we need to confirm the boys' identity?"

"Sure, both boys are my pupils at the Boarding School over there, no problem!"

The ambulance rushes towards a hospital nearby with the boys reasonably comfortable after the gruesome, violent attack.

The night passes without further incident apart from Dileep vomiting in his bed confirming a very heavy concussion. Haleem, after receiving several sleeping tablets, spends a reasonably comfortable night considering the circumstances.

Mr. Sadeem gives the medical staff all the personal details pertaining to the boy's identity and, after visiting both, decides to return to his office at school to report the incident to the police, their parents and headmaster.

After several telephone calls and assurances that the boys will be OK, Mr. Sadeem swears to himself to catch the perpetrators of such a horrific crime, then flops onto his office sofa for a well-earned sleep.

Next morning, supporting two very painful headaches, the boys wake up and are confronted by local police who hope to extract enough information about their assailants because there have been several so-called 'Muslim-Gay-bashing' attacks in the park recently and before someone is murdered it would be advisable to catch the distorted thugs.

"Did you recognize any of the attackers?"

"No Sir, they were masked." Haleem answers.

"Were they adults or teenagers?"

"I believe teenagers sir because their voices were not adult."

"Could they be from your school, maybe you know them and maybe they followed you?"

"It is possible sir, Dileep and me have been teased and bullied, but we are taking lessons in martial arts, so lately they have left us alone!"

"Are you both Muslim boys?"

"Yes sir, and we are great friends, but I dance, act, and sing in many theatres here, and maybe they are jealous of my success, or just hate Muslims and believe Dileep and myself are homosexuals, I do not know!"

"OK, maybe we should interview some of the boys in your dormitory and inspect some cricket bats in the gymnasium because removing blood samples from wood tends to be difficult, and such brutal hooligans would not think of cleaning their fingerprints either! Well done and thank you, your information will help. We hope you have a good recovery, and we promise to do everything to find your attackers, sure!"

During the coming days Haleem's parents visit their son and he assures them everything is OK. Only a huge black, swollen eye and heavy headaches cause some discomfort. Dileep has no visitors from his family, only the headmaster, and Mr. Sadeem visit him to offer their solidarity. He will require a longer stay in the hospital because of a slight hemorrhaging in the skull and, of course, a heavy concussion. However, the specialists predict he will be OK and return to normal health.

In the interim local police visit the school and interview several boys who sleep in Haleem's dormitory. They discover several suspicious characters and ask them about their feelings towards Muslims in their Hindu majority school.

"We hate them!" three boys answer as the police take their fingerprints. Other boys answer, with slight resentment towards their Muslim colleagues, as the police ask them the same question, but there is no real aggression in their answers, just a general dislike especially if they believe that they could be gay too.

They then ask where all cricket bats are stored and, not to their surprise, discover several bats with blood stains on them. Albeit there was evidence of a feeble attempt to clean the bats,

"Typical teenagers," the police agents murmur to each other.

With evidence in their hands and the suspect boys' fingerprints, they leave the school. Three days later they return with sound evidence that the three who answered aggressively were also the boys who bullied Haleem and Dileep about their religion and sexuality.

Haleem, now slightly better, is transported to the police station to listen to the voices of the boys; hidden of course. He identifies the voices, and combined with blood samples and fingerprints, it seems the boys, suffer from a rather deep-sitting, perverted hate of all thing Muslim and gay, confirmed after several interviews with police psychiatrists. The boys attacked several Muslims, male and female, and homosexuals who frequent the park after dark.

After the horrific ordeal, Haleem, begins to become aware of the importance of his Muslim religion because unlike the other Hindu boys, wanting to become an entertainer in the Hindu world could have major problems.

He does not enjoy participating with other boys at sports because being a Muslim, and his only aim in life is to become a classical dancer, is a thing which many Muslims believe is better left to females!

The only real friend he has is Dileep, a Muslim too. Haleem regards this friendship as a brotherly thing and is grateful that such he has found such a nice boy who understands his ambitions to beat the world and fight against all odds to become famous in a very difficult, Hindu run world.

"So, what am I, and what will I become?" he asks himself, doubting as most teenagers entering puberty tend to do.

"I want to find out, so maybe I can have a chat with the school psychologist about these doubts relating to my religion and my sexuality because talking to my father about such things is impossible!" It is now time to sleep as Haleem is totally exhausted after his terrible ordeal.

During the next day, he made an appointment with the school psychologist, a lovely, ageing female, who helps boys through difficult periods during their boarding school periods; a most testing time for many.

He is not nervous at all as he approaches her study, although the night was quite a sleepless one after his recent, harrowing experiences. He knocks on the door,

"Haleem, dear boy, please enter, I have heard much about you and cannot wait to have a long chat with you." Mrs. Salina Singh says.

"Take a seat and tell me about yourself and why you desire to see me?"

Haleem begins to tell her about his desire to entertain, dance, act and sing. She nods in approval.

He then tells her about his awful experience being beaten up by a gang of Muslim-gay-bashers and how he just does not understand why they picked on him and his friend Dileep. She nods again already having knowledge of the incident.

She then asks him,

"Haleem, dear boy, you are a most talented young man, I know because I have read your files from Junior School and about your superb performances here in plays, musicals and theater appearances. You are a born entertainer, and sometimes talented entertainers in their early years are misunderstood by society in general. Our Indian society loves to discriminate and show ignorance to those who are blessed with such talents. This is a problem that you will be confronted with during your life. However, your eventual success will overwhelm such discrimination and, you must never give in to those who bully and insult you. They will eventually bow to your success and cheer you on."

"Dear Haleem, that is enough for today, go to the hospital and care for your friend Dileep, he needs your brotherly love and support. In addition, here is a book you should read, it is about an English entertainer called, Sir Cliff Richard, it is a biography about his life and will help a little more to understand about yourself, your religion, feelings, and your desires because he was confronted by a similar situation in the UK.

Sir Cliff was born of Indian descent, a Muslim, and became popular in the UK sixties pop movement by imitating US rock-and-roller, Elvis Presley. Later in his life he reverted to Christianism, and when he became famous, many tabloids queried his Muslim background and sexuality. Dear boy this was way back when in the sixties! Muslims in the UK were virtually unheard of, in fact, British children only knew of the Islamic religion through stories of King Richard and his slaughtering, barbaric crusades in the Middle East being depicted as national heroes, like the Raj here in India!

We live here in our region in a Hindu majority and Muslims tend to be ignored, rather 'swept under the carpet' and, basically do not exist in the eyes of many. So, please read his biography carefully and learn from him that one does not have to be forced into any religious direction or divulge one's sexual preference if one does not desire just like Sir Cliff.

Even under tremendous public pressure he always maintained that he was only responsible to one God, and once he reverted to believing in Jesus you can imagine how his

Muslim parents felt! His religious belief supported his public image. He vowed that God, a Christian God, would lead him into being whatever he was destined to be and that is something you must also decide. Can you become what you want to be and be accepted by the Hindu majority here in the region and, is that important for you?!"

You, Haleem, will later become famous and this book will help to teach you how difficult life can be as a famous personality. Please read and study Sir Cliff's life and it will help you later in your daily life whilst being confronted with tabloids, paparazzi and other hyenas prying into your private life. Never bow to their demands and always remain what you are because there is only one person you must be true too, that is yourself! Now run along and we will speak same time, same day, next month. Enough for now and please stay clear of that damn park in the evening, it is not a nice place to be for such a talented, good-looking, young chap like yourself."

"Madam, how did you know about my troubles in the park?"

"Dear boy, these walls have ears, and eyes, and we know much more than you young chaps believe, now run along and start to enjoy what God has given you, a blessed talent that only a very few possess!"

"Thank you, Madam, I feel much better and now it is time to visit my dear friend Dileep; I do hope he is recovering after that shocking attack."

"He is, do not worry!" She smiles as he leaves the room.

Life for a mega-talented, dance orientated, male teenager can be hard at times especially when those surrounding that person totally misunderstand why he or she is so different from the rest. However, this is a defining period in everybody's life; some navigate it with ease, others find it distressful, harrowing and even depressive.

After recent negative events occurring in Haleem's young life and his determination to search for the answers with the right people, it seems now that he is well on his way to overcoming the demons that attack us all and, a light at the end of the 'teenage ghost ride of horrors' is now appearing. He feels uplifted, confident, and determined to defeat any other confrontations with negative energies that surround many people. There is only one goal in his life, to perfect his talents and give millions of people much pleasure when entertaining them in the future.

He visits his dear friend Dileep finding him chirpy and upbeat after the horrific attack. They decide to avoid the park after dark because their attack spread like wildfire around the school and, although many pupils show total solidarity with them, others still tease and attempt to bully them, but bullies are now aware that the duo possess defensive, fighting skills and are very brave.

After leaving the hospital Haleem's mind is buzzing about what Mrs. Singh told him about Sir Cliff Richard. In his mind he accepted the fact that his religion in an area of Muslim minority would cause problems, but he was determined to fight those prejudices. However, being during puberty years, Sir Cliff's sexuality puzzled him and, being quite aware of other boys in the dormitory hiding images of half-naked Bollywood actresses under their mattresses, and masturbating (quite normal at that age), he had no desires at all to join the fun.

It was disturbing, and although he had his dear friend who was like a dear brother to him and they shared their lives, there was never any feelings of sexual attraction. So, Haleem began to doubt about his own sexuality because he loved being with girls but felt no 'twinges in his groin' they were just wonderful to be with and their common interests in dancing.

There was however one mathematics teacher who attempted to 'flirt' with him and offered after school lessons in his apartment. Haleem felt uncomfortable with the approaches of this teacher but thought it would be a good idea to find out more about him.

Other boys knew he was gay because they had spotted him entering the park at night alone and, they also knew many young prostitutes, male and female, hung around the park looking for a quick buck to earn.

That evening, Haleem decides to see if this teacher was on a nightly prowl and hides in one of the bushes on the periphery of the park, no luck, it wasn't his night.

He returns to his dormitory and swears to himself to hide until the teacher feels the need to enter the park.

Evening for evening, after dark, Haleem waits patiently out of sight. Three evening later, jackpot! His beloved mathematics teacher leaves his apartment and enters the park, Haleem follows, tense and shivering with fear.

The teacher enters a well-known hang-out area in the park where young boy/girl prostitutes offer their services. He stops and talks to one young teenage boy who is laughing and fooling around with his colleagues. The boy is wearing make-up and lipstick, Haleem observes from behind a huge banyan tree.

The boy nods and the teacher pulls out some rupee notes, hands it over to him, and they disappear into the bushes. Haleem breaks out in a cold sweat but is determined to see what the teacher and the boy are doing. He slips around the back of the area where the teacher and boy went. A few yards in front of him in a small clearing, the teacher, and the boy prostitute, are doing something that sends waves of fear through Haleem's body.

He nearly becomes physically sick at the sight and runs away breathing heavy and sweating profusely. The sight of the teacher having sex with the boy was revolting and, on the way back to his dormitory Haleem swears he would never, ever participate in such a vulgar act!

Haleem leaps on his bed with his mind still spinning at the awful sight he just witnessed. He rapidly searches for the book Mrs. Singh gave him about Sir Cliff Richard's life and the chapter where he explains his sexuality.

Calming down, Haleem begins to read Sir Cliff's explanation about why he never married a female, and what were his reasons for remaining a virgin for all his life. The reasons given were, Sir Cliff was of the opinion being a strict Christian, he would never participate in sex before marriage anyway. Secondly, Sir Cliff, in his early years, never especially felt attracted to females of males so he remained A-sexual meaning no sexual preference or desire to have sex.

Haleem stops after reading these explanations, his heart is still beating heavily, but now, in his early teens has discovered why he isn't like many of the other boys of his age.

He contemplates and analyses his situation,

"I feel no urge to masturbate and certainly no urge to get physically involved with my dear friend Dileep. I love the presence of girls but feel no urge to flirt or touch them either. This means I am like Sir Cliff, A-sexual, thank the heavens for that," he gasps with relief.

"Form now on I will concentrate purely on achieving my goals, to become a classical dancer like Billy Elliot, and a film actor and entertainer. Nothing else will get in my way and it is my destiny that I witnessed my depraved mathematics teacher, and that dreadful boy having sex, something I never want to witness again. My life from now on will only consist of schoolwork and, dedication to becoming a Kuchipudi dancer at the highest level. Until I reach and, achieve my goals, there will be no time for flirting with girls or boys because I have no interest in both anyway, my luck!"

Haleem, mentally exhausted after such an experience, falls into a deep sleep and dreams about wonderful, colorful Kuchipudi dancers, male and female and from now on will dream about nothing else, especially sex, but maybe when he's older and an adult that might change; who knows?

His final year at secondary school is dedicated solely to achieving the necessary diplomas that will earn him the right to enter either a classical dance, or acting academy. At this moment in time, it matters not in which direction the warm Indian breezes will blow him. First, he must qualify at secondary school level, then he can choose with the help of his qualifications, what the next step will be. For the time being it is head down into the tedious work of studying subjects required to achieve enough diplomas, so he can achieve his goal and, to please his family of course.

Haleem and Dileep continue to study Marshall Arts under the steady guidance of Mr. Sadeem, which will give them both additional confidence whilst dealing with life and difficult situations that could occur. But for the time being, Haleem has vowed to steer clear of danger by avoiding nocturnal walks in parks with his dear friend Dileep. A harsh lesson into how brutal life can be has been learned; sure!

Chapter five

Some things in life are not coincidental

After a final semester of hard studying with hardly any free time to pursue his hobbies; dancing, acting, and generally entertaining, Haleem reaches the point of no return. In the presence of his very proud parents, he receives his diplomas from the Boarding School headmaster in the annual ceremony reserved for those who have been successful and, totally dedicated.

He walks up on to the stage to huge applause from everybody in attendance (they are all aware of the multi-talented young man standing in front of them) to collect his diplomas. He waves to the crowd, thanks his teachers, especially Mrs. Singh and Mr. Sadeem for their wonderful support in a final difficult year.

Fortunately, the brutal nightmare in the park never repeated itself, and now decisions are to be made into which university the son of Mehutai and Rasheed Khan will enter.

Mr. and Mrs. Khan stand proudly watching their very popular son, who has entertained hundreds of spectators during many musicals, theatre pieces and plays in his years at the school. It is a sad moment for many seeing him leave, but Haleem will always play a fond role in the hearts of many teachers and pupils who were lucky to witness such a talented child pass through their school.

Dileep stands with a tear in his eye knowing that the two of them must go in different directions because he has chosen a university in the north of India to study human rights, Mumbai to be exact.

"Dileep, dear friend we will maintain contact and maybe later I will be arriving in Mumbai anyway to pursue my career within theatre or films, who knows? So, we will meet up again, sure, but first I have other things to do, and sadly, I must remain in Hyderabad."

Listening to the two boys saying goodbye, Haleem's parents could not help but overhear what he said to Dileep.

"Dear son, we will talk about that at home, no decision has been made as too your future, but one thing is sure, we must be certain that the next step is one that will drive you forward into a successful career! After all, your mother and I are financing your life, so we have some serious talking to do, but do not worry, and let us celebrate your academic success here first!" Haleem's father sternly says.

"Father, my life is mine and nothing you or the family can or will ever do can stop me from achieving my destiny and goal in life. I wish nothing else than to become an entertainer. I have been given a godly gift and nobody will hinder me in fulfilling my dream. Academic success is only a means to an end and now it is time for me to search for a place where they can help me fine-tune my talents. This is what I will do, with you or without you!" Haleem replies.

"This is not the place to discuss such things, let us go home and enjoy the moment and then we can discuss your future, deal?"

"OK, dear father, but please do not attempt to hinder me in any manner because I know now what I will. It is my destiny to give great pleasure to thousands! One day you and the family will be very proud of my achievements!"

Haleem's mother listening to the rather heated conversation walks over to him, kisses him on his cheek, the left one, and whispers in his ear,

"Dear Haleem, do not worry about your silly dad, I know what you desire, and you my boy will get all the support necessary to achieve your ambitions, sure!"

Huge crocodile tears run down Haleem's and his mother's cheeks as they hold hands and hug each other.

"Thank you, dear mother, my love for you is eternal and, wherever I go, and whatever I achieve, you will always be with me and dad of course, but that might take a bit more time before he accepts my destiny!"

Both burst out laughing acknowledging Haleem's astute judgement of the situation pertaining to his dad and both are very amused as Haleem's father stares at the happy pair wondering what is causing so much amusement!

They say goodbye to everybody concerned at the school. Haleem gives his dear friend Dileep a final, huge bear hug, manly style, and then they head for a taxi waiting to take them back to Ongole for celebrations.

Haleem's father, Rasheed, sits in the taxi silently pondering over the comments that his son made to him. Mehetai and Haleem just chat about school, laugh, are extremely happy and, proud of his academic achievements in very difficult circumstances after hearing of the bullying and terrorization that happened.

Those times are now over, and the whole family can look forward to a bright future for Haleem, except for Rasheed, who is doubting about his son's intentions to enter an artistic based school instead of pursuing a 'proper' career.

They arrive home and the whole family is waiting to greet Haleem after his academic success; granddad, grandma, uncles and aunties arrive for a typical Andhra Pradesh high tea hoping to find out what the next step will be in their talented family member's career.

"Haleem, dear boy, congratulations, I guess you will be now heading to Bangalore or Mumbai to one of the country's best universities, sure?" Granddad inquires.

"Sir, I have not yet decided where to go, but I do desire to pursue a career in the artistic, entertainment world, maybe I can stay near in Hyderabad, there is an art academy there and my art teacher has written a recommendation for me!"

"That would be fantastic Haleem, but what does your father think about your intentions?"

"I guess his intentions for me are far away from those that I desire, I do not wish to disappoint him, but it is my life, and I must attempt to satisfy the urges within me and hope that I succeed. At school, I entertained many people, acting and dancing, this gave me great pleasure, now I must perfect my skills and natural born talent, and Hyderabad seems a good step forward Sir, sure."

"My, son, it is not the time and place to discuss this very sensitive subject, let us enjoy your celebrations and, after a couple of days talk about which direction you should take!" Rasheed, listening to the conversation butts in quite agitated, but he manages to keep his doubts and worries over his son hidden in front of the family, especially granddad who seemingly is in support of his son's rather eccentric desires.

The celebrations continue into the early evening as guests begin to leave wishing Haleem all the best for his future not quite aware of a potential rift between father and son appearing on the horizon. Rasheed and Mehetai wave goodbye to the final guests as Haleem, after a very tiring day, retires into his bedroom. He thanks his parents once again for their patience and support and wishes them both a good night's rest. He enters the bedroom, places a pair of newly acquired headphones over his ears and listens to the soothing music entering his mind; classical Kuchipudi music, knowing that this traditional, classical Indian dance music will play a very important part of his future life. He falls asleep and dreams of becoming a Kuchipudi dancer like many times before in his dreams. His only ambition is to entertain thousands of people all over India and maybe the world. A dream that is not quite in the future plans of his father, but that's another bridge to be crossed in the sometimes-troubled life of this multi-talented young man.

Chapter six

Hyderabad, the beginning of it all

Two days later, after dinner, Haleem retires to his bedroom then Rasheed knocks on his door and enters:

"Haleem, we must discuss this problem, there is no point in hiding our feelings! I want you to go and learn a suitable career, and with your academic qualifications, I am sure you can become a successful doctor, lawyer, or a top manager in a global company. However, you must study first in Bangalore or Mumbai, then go abroad to perfect your English in an English or American university. We are prepared to support you as much as we can financially, and your grandparents are also willing to invest in their grandson. We have family in the US and UK, so it will not be a problem sending you over there, but first you must rid your mind of this foolish idea about becoming an entertainer of some sort. Your mother, the family, and I are not prepared to invest our hard-earned savings into such a risky and, if you ask me personally, foolish idea!"

"Sir, I respect your wisdom, but no! Absolutely no! There is only one thing I desire, that is to become an entertainer. I do not know in which art form or direction my ambitions will take me, but a career in industry, law, medicine, or anything else but the arts and entertainment, is impossible. If you and the family do not support me then I will find a way to support myself, I do not care. That is my final word, and with all respect, I refuse to discuss the subject further!" Haleem replies in a determined, but respectful manner because being rude to parents in India is absolute taboo and if children are disrespectful or rude to their parents, the consequences can be very uncomfortable.

"We shall see what the consequences are over your ambitions but believe me my son your attitude and fantasy life will lead to a disaster and great disruption in the family, especially between your mother and me because I know she shows much sympathy towards you, that is natural, but I do not. I only want the best for my son, and I know this rather foolish ambition will cause massive problems between us, you have been warned!"

"Father, dear father, I respect and love you dearly Sir, but this is my life, and I must do what I desire with my life, sorry. I am not prepared to sacrifice my ambitions to satisfy your desires and, as I mentioned, with your support or without it, I will do what I have to do and that is to follow my drive and ambitions!"

"OK, Haleem, have it your way, you have six weeks to decide where you want to go and maybe now you are back home you will realize how much your mother and myself have done already. This hopefully, will help you rid your mind of such thoughts! I sincerely hope so because your future will be decided here with us together and not by yourself."

"Sorry sir, you are wrong, my future is mine, and I will pursue my career the way I feel is correct for me and not to be responsible for how you or the family feels or believes! I apologize once again, but I wish to continue to perfect my artistic talents here in Hyderabad and nothing will stop me. This is my final word on the subject sir, so please, I am very tired and need to sleep, goodnight!"

Rasheed reluctantly leaves Haleem's bedroom, angry and bitter because he cannot convince his son of the importance of a 'sensible' career. Mehetai sits quietly in the living room knitting. However, these thin walls have ears and, she obviously heard everything that was spoken!

"Darling Rasheed, forget it, you will not force Haleem to do anything he does not want to do! He is an extremely talented artist, look at his reports and study his recommendations to enter an artistic academy! Then you will discover how driven and ambitious he is and not foolish like you accuse him of being! He will succeed with your support or without it. The problem is not Haleem, it is you, so you better take a long look at yourself in the mirror before you lose the love and respect of your only son."

"You, you, all you do is give in to him! All his life you have supported his strange habits and character. Now at the most important part of his life you bow to his demands again! Sorry, this has gone too far, and I refuse to support Haleem any further unless he realizes that this world is not built upon fantasy; it is built upon hard work and, learn, learn, learn! This is the only way to success and not to become some dancer or actor in a fantasy world. If you support him then we will also have a problem because he is a young man, a young Muslim man, and in the real world out there, things are difficult enough, let alone attempting to become a dancer or actor! Don't you understand Mehetai, or are you just another stupid Muslim woman who does not understand the world as we men do?"

"Rasheed, calm down, no more insults or we will really have a problem, I maybe a Muslim woman, but I am not stupid, and I do know one thing, Haleem will work hard, study and become what he desires. He will surprise you in your narrow world, and then, and only then, will you see how wonderful your son really is! Now this is enough nonsensical talk, I am tired too, tired of your foolishness!"

She storms out of the room leaving Rasheed in a terrible dilemma between anger and doubt. However, there is no way he will budge on his decision. Haleem must make it on his own and in no way will the family support him!

As another domestic storm settles above the Khan family residence, Haleem, sits in his room quietly listening to his favorite music that accompanies his favorite classical Indian dance, Kuchipudi. It soothes his mind as his father's threats buzz between his rather disturbed brain. However, determination is everything and after all it is his life. Come what may, support or no support, he will certainly be going to the art Academy in Hyderabad, and any thought of attending law school, an IT university, or joining the medical world is impossible.

The summer recession passes without too many difficulties because father and son, separated by mum, hardly speak. Haleem then attends an invitation from the Hyderabad Art/ Acting Academy after receiving recommendations from his Boarding School with outstanding references and, the necessary academic qualifications; just.

He is welcomed by the head professor and revered classical dance teacher, Guru Sri K.V Subrahmanyam, an Indian renowned master of classical dance.

"Haleem, dear boy we have heard much about you, I have also had the pleasure of seeing your performances on video sent to me by your mentor in Boarding School and we wish to offer you a three-year scholarship in classical dance, acting, and music. We feel you have a great future in these art forms and wish to support you. However, one thing is sure, you must also, parallel to your artistic talents, complete a certain level of academic qualification here. We educate our students in the arts, but do expect them to leave here with a reasonable command of basic subjects just in case you fail to progress in the world of theatre, acting, or entertainment, is that clear?"

"Yes sir, sure, it is very clear, and I am most honoured to have this opportunity to enter your prestigious academy, but I do have one minor problem, my father refuses to finance my studies because he wishes me to enter a 'sensible career'. So, if I may be so prudent as to ask; is there any possibility to arrange some form of finance through external avenues?"

"Dear Haleem, this problem occurs very often where strict parents, especially fathers, attempt to force their male offspring to enter solid careers, especially those of Muslim religion like your father's. They regard any form of entertainment as being rather absurd, useless, and degrading for the family. I will do my very best to organise finances for your scholarship because in your special case, the potential for you to enter the world of classical dance, theatre and acting are enormous. We as a renowned Indian academy do not wish to lose such a precious talent, so do not worry and leave the finance problems to me."

"Dear Sir, I wish to thank you from the bottom of my heart and promise to do everything in my power to return your support, sure!" Haleem stands proudly in front of Guru Sri K.V Subrahmanyam, they shake hands, and he floats out of the office on a magical carpet!

A few weeks later a letter arrives in Haleem's house from the academy. Luckily, his father is at work as his mother gathers up the letter with tears in her eyes hoping it is the thing that will open the world for her talented son giving him a fantastic opportunity to fulfil his dreams. She brings the letter to Haleem, who is listening to Ravi Shankar sitar music in his room. She shows him the letter, shaking. Haleem also begins to shake and enters into a state of total apprehension as he dares not to open the letter. He begins to perspire; his hands shake as he begs his mother to open the letter. She agrees and reaches for a pair of scissors lying on the table that she uses whilst embroidering, and repairing holes in socks, a common thing in Indian households, holes in socks.

Her uncontrollable hands slit open the letter and, she unfolds it.

Haleem, with tears swelling in his eyes cannot look, so he covers them with his moist, sweaty, vibrating hands.

"Please Mama reveal to me what is in the letter, I cannot wait a second longer! The excitement grows as Mehetai nearly faints,

"Dear Haleem, they have accepted you and are offering a financial package that you should reimburse later!!"

They leap into each other's arms, crying and jumping for joy!

"What is going on here?" A stern voice from the living room enters the fray after returning from a day's work at the office.

"Rasheed, Haleem has been offered a scholarship at the Hyderabad Art/Acting Academy, is this not fantastic news? In addition, we do not have to pay one rupee because he is receiving government financial support in the form of an interest free credit that only must be reimbursed if he succeeds and enters the art, classical dancing, or acting world. Are you not happy for your son?"

Rasheed storms out of the house without saying a word leaving his ecstatic wife and son to enjoy one of the most important moments in his and her life. Haleem's father thinks otherwise as he rapidly walks to the local mosque searching for an answer to calm his rage and anger through praying to Allah.

He enters the mosque hoping to find the local Imam who is busy preparing evening prayer.

"Sire, I have an immense problem, my son Haleem has been given a scholarship at the Art/Acting Academy in Hyderabad and I refuse to accept this because he must enter a proper college or university and not fool around with such nonsense!"

"Dear Rasheed, I am aware of this problem in your household. I am also aware of the disruption this decision is causing between you and your beloved wife. She confided in me and divulged to me your stubbornness. The anger you feel subjective, your fears for your son are your fears and not his. Haleem is a wonderfully gifted young man and not what you desire him to be. His spirit is his own and nothing you can do will change that. You do not own your son; he is only given to you for a short period in his long life and, at one time you must let loose.

Dear Rasheed, curb your anger and rage, accept your son for what he is and, stop this foolishness, otherwise you will destroy your relationship with him and of course, your beloved wife. Only God will decide which career Haleem will take and the chances of him fulfilling his ambitions are very good with his god given talents. Swallow your anger, accept that he has his life and you yours, then everything will come good if you believe in the will of god, Allah, the great one!"

"Dear Imam, I thank you for your wise words. I guess I must follow the words of a wise man, swallow my anger and allow Haleem to live his own life, it will be utmost difficult, but with the strength of Allah I will do my best to accept this situation, thank you sir!"

Rasheed kisses the outstretched hand of the Imam and kneels towards Mecca to pray for guidance.

The rest of the summer recess passes with much silence between father and son. Mealtimes become quite strenuous with Rasheed refusing not to talk about his son's decision and only discussing the bare necessities. While Rasheed is at work, Haleem, and his mother, discuss his first exciting year at the academy. She also vows secretly to support him with the help of his grandparents. From her side of course. Haleem refuses to accept any help and is determined to fulfil his ambitions on his own.

"Don't be foolish son, my parents and I will make sure you are cared for properly, in fact, we have family in Hyderabad, and they will gladly arrange accommodation for you, so do not worry!" Mehetai says.

"But mother, with all respect, I will receive government funding very soon, and I sincerely wish to do this thing on my own!"

"No! If you refuse my offer then you will not only have a problem with your foolish father, do you understand me?"

"OK, Mother, I accept your support, but only if the accommodation is for me alone and not with the family. I want to be free to express myself in any way I desire and do not wish the hawk-eyes of your family following my every move! Is that a deal?"

"Sure, I will tell the family in Hyderabad to locate a room for you whilst you study and will also tell them to leave you alone, no problem!"

"Fantastic mother, now I can commence my journey to riches and fame, and I will make sure the whole family, including dad, will be very proud of me one day! I thank you so much!"

Haleem pulls his dear mother to him and gives her a huge loving hug. She weeps for joy knowing that her beloved son is so happy. However, deep inside she feels a sadness because she knows that this parting of the ways will mean her loving son will never actually return to the family, except on visits; it's a maternal thing, sure!

Chapter seven

Strange encounters of a third kind

Many times, the atmosphere in Haleem's house becomes quite unbearable although Rasheed attempts desperately to abide by his religious leader's advice. Such evenings become quite hectic and force Haleem to escape to his bedroom.

One-night, Haleem lies restless in his bed after yet another argument with his beloved father. He then slips out of the house. It is 23.00 PM as wonderful aromas floating upon a warm breeze from Banyan trees and orchids reach his nostrils calming the agony of a seemingly irreparable situation between him and his father.

He wanders aimlessly through the dark, back streets of Ongole not seeing or perceiving anything apart from the inner pain inflicted upon him by his father.

He enters a huge open area where locals dump their rubbish and unwanted possessions. It used to be a huge cement factory long abandoned after English companies, seeing no future in the Indian economy uprooted, counted their losses, and went back to the UK.

He walked through the open, abandoned area, usually visited, and inhabited by groups of stray dogs yowling with hunger and scrounging for morsels of anything edible among the plastic waste and rubbish. Normally, the yowling of stray dogs could be heard for miles and, although the locals accepted their unwelcome neighbors, they did not welcome them.

Haleem stopped and thought,

"Why is it so silent here tonight? Normally yowling dogs could be heard from a great distance, but tonight they are silent."

He carried on, stumbling now and then over protruding pieces of sharp rusting iron embedded in hardened cement left by their past owners,

"Damn Brits," he thinks.

Hardly seeing anything in the darkness in front of him, he decides his long walk was enough to calm his feelings. So, he turns and heads back in the direction of home. After walking several paces, the sound of slurping and licking reaches his ears coming from behind a battered, graffiti ridden wall, which once was the gatehouse to the factory, but now only used by tramps, stray dogs, and other nocturnal, homeless creatures.

The noise reaching his ears arouses his interest. Haleem decides to peek inside the derelict remains. A dim, torch light can be seen shimmering in the dark as he approaches the gap where once a huge iron door stood. He stops and stares into the rays of the torchlight that suddenly shines upon him. The canine inhabitants in the building ignore his presence because they are too hungry and busy enjoying their evening meal.

"Hey, you, what are you doing here at this ungodly time, and with whom do I have the pleasure?"

The person holding the torch turns continues to flash the narrow beam of light into Haleem's face,

"Is it any of your business what I am doing? Moreover, if you wish to leave this place in one peace, please do not disturb my canine friends while they are enjoying their evening meal!"

"By the way my name is Kelly Johnson, who the hell are you, and what the hell do you think you are doing spying on me? Are you one of those despicable dog haters who make my life so difficult by threatening me with violence and kick and beat my friends here?"

"Please, no madam, my name is Haleem Khan, I was just wandering through the night after a desperate argument with my dad, a thousand apologies madam, I am very sorry. However, please tell me what you are doing with these stray dogs, I am most interested as nobody else in Ongole seems to care about them. They mostly end up as glue in the local glue factory or on the plates of those dreadful Chinese monsters!"

"Ha, ha, so you are aware of the way your people treat these poor, starving animals? Well, my colleagues and myself, feed the dogs at night, we give them medical care in the daytime and, treat them like they deserve to be treated. Not like most Indians treat them! They may not be holy cows, but they are living creatures and we attempt at least to save as many as possible from starvation or being beaten to death by locals who cannot sleep at night because of the yowling. We fight against dog-hunters paid by the government who catch them and cull them mercilessly. My organization is saving stray dogs in Southern India, helping them to find a home and, attempting to reduce their numbers in a humane way through sterilization. They are not holy cows, they are dogs who were originally abandoned by their owners, left to their own devices, and have multiplied in numbers. Something they cannot help doing, it's a natural thing you know, called multiplication! So, we sterilize them in a humane manner to halt their rapidly growing numbers. Local councils employ people to hunt the dogs and sterilize them without anesthetics; a dreadful, painful and harmful process"

"Kelly, you have my respect, and when you have finished your obligations this evening, please let me accompany you home, I wish to know more about your organization and, when I have time, I would love to help. By the way where do you come from with that strange accent?"

"Give me five minutes and I'll be finished here, then we can walk together. By the way what is your name again?"

"Haleem Khan madam."

"Please to meet you Haleem."

"Sure!"

"In answer to your question, I am half English and half German, hence my slight accent. I have resided in India for five years now, and you?"

"I am about to leave Ongole because I have earned a scholarship at the prestigious art academy in Hyderabad. Being a Muslim, my dad will just not accept my decision to pursue a career in dance, acting and entertainment generally. But my story is long so let us first walk home and maybe one day we can exchange our stories if you wish to?"

They leave the derelict building together chatting and talking. Kelly tells Haleem how she came to India following a love affair that sadly did not last and, Haleem tells Kelly his story and the reason for his sadness. Within an hour it seems they have known each other for ever. They reach Kelly's house and sit outside in the warm air chatting, laughing, and enjoying each other's company. It appears this friendship was destined to happen between two so diverse, misunderstood and, totally different characters. They both listen and tell their quite different life stories.

Kelly, then divulges a secret that only her dearest friends and family know; her battle against breast cancer and how she defeated it. Haleem sits mesmerized by this fascinating female character, who has had a difficult background just like himself.

"Haleem, believe me, you can defeat any problem if you have the ambition and will to do it. After listening to your difficult story, childhood, problems with your Muslim background, your desires and of course, the anger with your father, I feel we can help each other!"

"Kelly, I believe this meeting was meant to be, I believe in destiny and that you have crossed my path is our destiny, I feel like I have met a long-lost sister who understands me, gives me strength through her determination, your willingness to confront and defeat any problem, no matter how huge. Thank you, Kelly, you are my guiding angel!"

"Haleem, please, I am no angel, I am just a normal European lady with a heart for those who maybe experience life in a slightly more difficult manner than I do. Although I have defeated my cancer, the fight continues and meeting you, with your background, also gives me strength to enjoy your company, so can we meet again?"

"Sure, Kelly, I will come around tomorrow evening to assist you with your work and, before I leave for Hyderabad to join the Art Academy, I hope we can help each other, of that I am sure!"

"I will look forward to that and hope to see you tomorrow evening. Maybe for dinner before we go out to feed my doggies, good night, Haleem, it was wonderful meeting you!"

They shake hands as Kelly enters her house. Haleem heads back home feeling wonderful and relieved after this most unusual meeting of a 'third kind'.

In the coming weeks Kelly and Haleem meet regular giving each other support by exchanging their life-changing experiences. Haleem helps Kelly and her colleagues to care for stray dogs showing utter admiration for the voluntary work they do. It gives him strength and fills him with even more ambition to achieve his goal. He also vows never to forget Kelly as their friendship becomes stronger by the day because Kelly must return to Bangalore to continue her work there, saving stray dogs and, working together with local vets in humane castration projects.

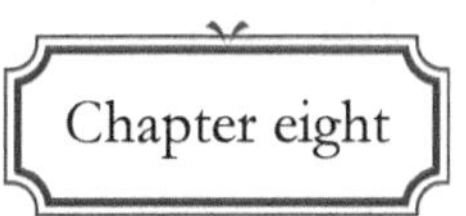

Chapter eight

Departures can be hard, but some are easier

The day of departure arrives, mid-September, and luckily things are gradually drying out after the annual monsoon rains pass over the region leaving the air moist, warm, and quite pleasant. Haleem, stands at the door with his mother and sister crying tears of great sadness, combined with joy, a difficult scenario. Haleem's father, still stubborn and quite angry, leaves for work as usual without saying goodbye to him or wishing him luck. He turns his back and exits the gate leaving Haleem with a feeling of deep sadness and regret.

Hopefully things will change in the future, as he does not hold a grudge against his father at all and is determined to win the affection of his dad back by proving him wrong.

His huge brown eyes swell with tears as Haleem thinks to himself,

"Dad, I love you with all my heart, but my future is mine, not yours and one day soon you will find a way to overcome your anger and doubts, so we can become one again, even if it needs heavenly intervention!"

Rasheed, head hung deep, rushes to the train station holding a handkerchief to his nose whilst tears run down his cheeks.

He meets some colleagues from work.

"Rasheed, dear chap, what's the matter? Is it about Haleem leaving and are you still angry with him?" One of them ask.

"Foolish man, my eyes are running because of the damn moisture in the air, I feel like I am contracting hay fever, nothing else, sure!"

His colleagues pat him on the back hoping that he will feel better when he reaches work, but deep inside they know the truth behind Rasheed's red eyes and tearful situation; the lesser said the better.

Haleem enters the train station an hour later accompanied by his mother, sister, and his new-found friend, Kelly, who is also leaving for Bangalore. He gets ready to board the local train from Ongole to Hyderabad. He has a sturdy, ancient leather suitcase in his hand lent to him by his granddad; his mother's hand rests in the other. The train stands idling ready to depart, they hug once more, mother, sister, and Haleem. Tears fill the eyes of his mum and sister, Haleem's too.

Kelly stands admiring the love shown between Haleem and his mother and sister. A tear of emotion runs down her cheek as she thinks of her family faraway in Europe. Haleem goes over to her and asks why she is so upset.

"Kelly, my dear new-found friend please tell me what the matter is, are you going to miss me, please, I am not that far away, and you can come to Hyderabad any time!" He smiles and gives her a huge hug.

"Good luck Haleem, and although I will miss you very much it is not the reason I am upset. In fact, I am so happy for you, and I will come to visit you in your new life, do not worry. My tears fall because I feel the love between you and your mum and sister. As you know I have a Mum, Dad, his lovely wife, three brothers, a wonderful sister-in-law, plus a wonderful niece and, although I adore India, I miss them very much. Please do not worry, it happens when I see families being happy and loving to each other. However, my present life here means much to me, but one day I will return, no doubt, because I know my family only want one thing, for me to return. But I have time and things to do here just like you have things to do in Hyderabad; now get on that train! Enough of this emotional nonsense!"

He then turns to the train, jumps on board, pulls down the next available window, blows kisses to them and waves as the ancient, built in Scotland many years ago, steam engine, shunts slowly towards Haleem's future. He is filled with mixed emotions of joy and sadness, but deep inside he knows that this is the biggest and correct step in his life and will not look back.

The steam engine exits the station as Mehetai, and Haleem's sister exit the busy station feeling left quite alone. Kelly comforts them, say's her goodbyes and waits for the train to Bangalore.

Although Haleem stayed at that horrible boarding school for three years, this time his parting is different, but that's life and his show must go on, it is his destiny.

Haleem sits down on his second-class seat with great expectations ringing between his ears. In addition, the thought of entering this wonderful academy on a super scholarship fills him with so much joy, he bursts out into song and hums his favorite Kuchipudi tunes nearly all the way to Hyderabad, apart from when he drinks a cup of lukewarm, very sweet tea, given to him by a passing tea-lady. Fellow passengers sit and enjoy the gentle, soothing music surrounding the compartment. Haleem just smiles to himself living in his world of song, dance, and entertainment mildly enjoying the admiring smiles of other travelers.

Nothing or nobody can take away a sense of utter satisfaction as the huge smoking, pre-World War 2 engine, rumbles through the green, fertile, Andhra Pradesh countryside towards his future destiny,

"First Hyderabad, then Mumbai, and then the rest of the world!" He thinks, smiles, and commences to sing once again!

The train arrives at Hyderabad main station as Haleem withdraws a scribbled piece of paper given to him secretly by his mother containing the address of a cousin of his mother who offered a spare room for a reasonable price. After all this is India and everybody must earn a rupee or two even if its family involved.

He calls a rickshaw, shows the driver the paper and leaps on board. Slaloming through crowds of people, cars, motorbikes, bicycles, and oxen-pulled carts loaded with anything sellable, the rickshaw makes its way slowly from the station to the address located in a middle-class suburb outside of the city. Fortunately, it is quite near the Art Academy and as the rickshaw passes the wonderful building built by the British during the

Raj, Haleem's blood begins to tingle and pump rapidly through his heart.

"This is where I belong among other great artists, musician, dancers, actors, and entertainers. I will prove to my dad that this decision is so correct, sure!"

The rickshaw pulls up in front of a huge metal gate surrounded by a high wall keeping those who are unwanted outside, and those inside, safe from the less fortunate who can only dream about owning such a villa.

Haleem's mother's cousin married a successful Indian entrepreneur who owns a chain of shops in the city and other cities, selling ironmongery products to their customers.

He rings the rusty, iron bell and the front door opens. Neha, Mehetai's cousin, appears dressed in a designer silk sari looking very impressive. She smiles and presses a button that opens the electronically controlled gate. Haleem enters and kisses Neha on the hand thanking her for the opportunity to reside in their prestigious villa.

She answers, "Dear boy, we have heard all about your talents and just cannot wait to see you soon in the theatres of Hyderabad. So, please feel at home as we fully support your ambitions, contrary to your stubborn father!"

She smiles, Haleem laughs and feels at home straight away. They proceed to his room situated on the top floor at the back of the house overlooking a fabulous garden being trimmed with pedantic, loving care by the gardener.

"Madame Neha, it is fabulous and just what I require for my studies, thank you and your dear husband so much for this opportunity!"

"Dear Haleem, no emotions right now, you have a hard three years in front of you and we will do anything to support you. Now freshen up as high tea will be served in the garden in thirty minutes. My husband will be home soon to have a chat with you about school, your dreams, and ambitions!"

"Thank you once again, I am so happy and determined to pay back your kindness and understanding through my future success. I will make the whole family very proud that I promise!"

She exits the room as Haleem flings himself on the huge, comfortable bed, feeling very happy and filled with high expectations!

The following Monday, Haleem approaches the huge granite stairway of the Hyderabad Art Academy for the first time. Standing at the top of the stairs is, Professor Shri Kaza Venkata Subramanyam garu, waiting to welcome his latest multi-talented pupil into the academy.

"Dear Haleem, we are so excited to welcome you into our prestigious establishment and cannot wait to develop your already superb talents. We have all the information about what you achieved at that dreadful Boarding School. That is all history and from now on you will have all the opportunities to learn every aspect of classical dance, acting, music and other forms of art. However, your basic studies must not be neglected as you know. So, it will mean much pleasure and very much hard work for the next three years; let's go, sure!"

They shake hands and Haleem follows the professor to a class filled with twenty other students, male and female, with similar talents. He enters the room; the pupils turn their heads and are taken aback by the obvious presence of a budding superstar. Haleem, slightly embarrassed by the stares quietly says,

"नमस्ते (Hallo)."

It breaks the ice immediately and then he takes his seat in the middle of the class sitting next to a wonderful looking young lady with huge brown eyes and long black eyelashes; he blushes. Sitting on the other side, a handsome young chap with a beautiful, purple-coloured silk turban sitting proudly on his Sikh head and, a perfectly trimmed beard, he blushes again!

Haleem's future mentor, Guru Sri K.V Subrahmanyam, stands in front of the class, greets all the students, and promises them that they will be allowed to express and perfect all their artistic talents in this wonderful academy. He also warns them again of the obligatory studies they must fulfil before achieving diplomas necessary for entrance into the entertainment world. If any students fail to uphold the academic side of academy expectations, their scholarship will be terminated. A dire warning for all students who believe that the Hyderabad Art Academy is an institution of pure pleasure and not for dedicated, hard workers!

It is a common fact that only a minor percentage of students attaining a scholarship at the academy achieve any form of success in the massive Indian entertainment industry. In addition, to enter the classical theatre world of dance, and performance, even more demands are expected among budding superstars regardless of their natural talent!

Haleem listens carefully to his mentor and silently vows to devote his entire life to becoming successful even if it means hours and hours of sweating over mathematic, geography, science, religious, or history books day and night.

"If this is the only way, then I will do it!" He swears to himself.

The curriculum is explained; times of study, arts, dance and acting lessons, strictly to be attended throughout the semester and homework to be completed in the evening. They all receive a copy of the curriculum and timetable. Books are issued pertaining to their studies.

After all the introductions, the students are dismissed to visit the different locations on the complex where diverse, active lessons in classical dance, music, acting, singing, painting, and other aspects of the art / entertainment world are taught.

Haleem feels the excitement grow in his limbs as he approaches the dance studio where a class of Kuchipudi dancers are being put through their paces. His heart races and beats profusely as he peers inside the studio.

Automatically, he feels a special affinity with this wonderful, classical art form. He becomes mesmerised by the fluent moves of the dancers, male and female. The new pupils then move on to the acting studio, but Haleem remains rooted to the ground marvelling at the dancers.

"Haleem, please move along, you will have plenty of time to participate in Kuchipudi classes, the choice is yours!" Guru Sri K.V Subrahmanyam calls.

He re-joins the class who are now inside the acting studio where future Bollywood and Tollywood stars first learn and perfect their skills.

"This academy is just amazing!" Haleem whispers to his new Sikh colleague.

"Sure is," he replies!

The female student who sat next to Haleem is also in ecstasy because her one desire in life is to become an actress. The trio admire an advanced acting class as they take on different roles masterfully slipping into Shakespearean 'Good, Bad, and Ugly' before their eyes.

"It's just like magic," Asha, the female student gasps!

"Sure is," Haleem replies.

The Sikh boy called, Kangkan, is also mesmerised by the superb performance because he also wishes to become an actor and dancer. They stand together in pure admiration hoping one day that they can perform to such high standards as this advanced class. Only time will tell!

Chapter nine

Time passes so fast when one is having fun!

It is inevitable that after such a short period attending the academy the raw, outstanding talents of Haleem become abundantly clear and, acknowledged by professors at the academy.

His first two years are a fantastic learning process and his fatal attraction towards the classical Indian dance, Kuchipudi, helps him to become a leading dancer in an advanced group that performs in front of huge audiences in the Hyderabad area and other major cities including Bangalore, Chennai, even Mumbai and Delhi.

The revered reputation of the school in Southern India gives students the opportunity to show their skills in front of mesmerised onlookers. Naturally, leading dancers, including Haleem, are particularly popular. Either dressed as a male or female. He wows the audiences no matter which venue the dance school performs.

Haleem's senior dance professor recognises the dedication and drive of this major talent and has no problems making the thriving, local entertainment, and theatre industry, aware of his pupil's quite outstanding talent.

Haleem's other artistic tangents also begin to develop at a very early phase in his studies, acting, comedy, theatre, singing, etc. The first two years just fly by, and we now enter his third and final year. A year of decision making that is also sad for the academy. The fact that they will be losing such an enormous talent dawns upon them. However, this fact belongs to their main targets, producing and refining raw talent.

Professor Guru Sri K.V Subrahmanyam arranges a massive show for parents and siblings at the end of the academy year before diplomas are handed out to the successful students. In addition, parallel to his artistic studies, Haleem is also reasonably successful in commanding his academic subjects too (with some slightly advantageous results given to him because of time required whilst representing the academy and, not too much time to study! But who cares? This is India and a once in a lifetime mega-talent like Haleem only appears once in a lifetime, logically, sure!).

The day of the final show arrives. Invited are not only parents, non-participating students, and siblings; Professor Guru Sri K.V Subrahmanyam has made sure many front seats are left vacant for talent scouts representing national Kuchipudi dance schools, film, and theatre organisations from all over India. Haleem's national reputation has grown and, it is now time for the prestigious academy to flaunt one of their best talents in front of some of the most renowned entertainment, classical and popular studios from all over India.

"Haleem, dear boy, this is your great day and after today the world will become your oyster! Out there are some of the most critical and renowned talent scouts from all walks of entertainment ready to offer you the possibility to go out and conquer the world, which I know you can do. So, go out there and WOW them with your talent!" Professor Guru Sri K.V Subrahmanyam tells Haleem.

"I will sir, I will, do not worry, after three years at your fabulous, prestigious academy, thanks to you, the other professors and teachers, I feel it is now time to progress even further and fulfil my ambitions!"

"You will my son, you will!"

Haleem is dressed in an astonishing, beautiful, silk, multi-coloured, female Kuchipudi outfit made especially for the show. The other dancers, male and female commence proceedings with a professional display of magical dance routines.

Then, entering the stage from the right, Haleem appears as the audience stand and applause. He proceeds with his mesmerising routine, leading the other dancers in a display of utter magic!

Sitting in the audience is of course Mehetai, Haleem's mother, and Rasheed, Haleem's father, who under protest, and threats of divorce from his wife, sits also mesmerised by the performance of his one and only son. Tears of pride run down his cheeks as he watches Haleem floating across the stage dancing elegantly and beautifully in wonderful synchronisation with his facial expressions, eyes, hands, and feet.

At last, Rasheed now knows after all these years of worry, torment, and anger, what his beloved son is destined to be! A deep feeling of satisfaction and utter happiness enters his mind as he observes the magic being performed before his eyes. He grasps Mehetai's hand shivering with pride and joy, they hug and kiss, and she says,

"See I told you Haleem one day would conquer the hearts of thousands, especially yours, the most important one he needed to conquer!"

Rasheed drops back into his chair as Haleem proceeds to wow the audience with one of the most difficult dance routines ever performed by the academy. Experts of the classical dance sit with mouths gaping open in astonishment as Haleem pulls off dance movements only reserved for those who have many more years of experience; he is a sensation!

The show ends. Then the whole cast enters centre stage to standing ovations, with of course, Haleem, standing and bowing proudly in the middle of it all. The whole audience rise to clap and cheer the cast. The head principle then enters with a microphone and attempts to calm the audience with a speech:

"Dear parents, pupils and others here tonight, you have just witnessed something that we as one of the most revered art academies in India never believed we could achieve, but anything is possible if you believe in it! Thanks to everybody involved, the teachers, professors, dancers and, one special thanks to our leading dancer, Haleem, an unbelievable talent of whom we know big, no, even huge things are planned! So, to all of you, enjoy the diploma presentations tomorrow and be very proud of your children leaving us. We hope they will all have a great future in whichever direction they go!"

The audience applauds again. Every dancer / performer receives a huge garland of flowers, they hold hands, bow and proudly march off; many with tears in their eyes, and not only the girls!

Haleem rushes to his mother and father, still dressed as a female, his mother gives him a huge hug and kiss. In the background, with proud tears streaming down his eyes, Rasheed stands, hoping that Haleem will forgive him for the misunderstood, sometimes horrid behaviour to his son over a period of many years. Haleem kisses his sister then approaches his dad,

"Dad, I am so happy you made it, I am so proud you saw me performing, and I sincerely hope you enjoyed the show?"

"Haleem, my one and only son, I am so sorry for my terrible ignorance and hope you will forgive me, I beg for your forgiveness, please!"

"Dad do not worry, the family has provided for me and helped me achieve so much and I will always be grateful to them. I hope now you will understand that your son, Haleem, is about to achieve and fulfil his dreams and ambitions. Dad, I hope your love for me and support for who and what I am, will never die. I love you so much and, of course I forgive you!"

They fall into each other's arms, both crying of course.

Then, from behind the happy couple, several talent scouts appear representing the prestigious Telegu film/entertainment company: Second only to India's globally famous, Bollywood studios.

"Dear Haleem, we wish to offer you the possibility to join our film, dance and acting groups. We represent, organise, and teach some of the greatest talents in India and wish to offer you a contract to join us so you can also develop your enormous talents with us! Please visit our Hyderabad office next week so we can sign the legal documents required especially suited to you!"

"Ladies and gentlemen, I am so grateful for this opportunity with your prestigious group and of course will be so happy to join such a wonderful list of performers. I am over the moon, and as you can see, my family are too!"

They shake hands, Haleem receives a visiting card from the CEO of the group given to him by one of the scouts with an appointment written on the back.

Tears roll down his eyes and his make-up begin to flow.

"Oh, ladies and gentlemen I do apologise, I guess it is time to change and get into my normal clothes but thank you all once again!"

They all smile at his politeness.

"Please Haleem feel free to change your outfit; we are sure we will recognise you dressed as a man next week!"

The whole crowd surrounding the group burst out laughing as Haleem scampers to his dressing room.

Chapter ten

A long weekend in Goa

After all the excitement, Haleem, feels the need to relax before his career officially begins the following week. So, he asks two friends to accompany him to Goa, a fabulous hippy-like beach resort for a long weekend. They spontaneously agree. However, Haleem being the gentle, kind person that he is, asks his friends if they mind if he invites a special friend along too, and of course they agree!

"Kelly, would you like to come to Goa for the weekend with myself and several friends before I start my career in Hyderabad with the Telugai entertainment company?"

He sends this E mail to his dear friend Kelly and of course she responds immediately with a huge, "yes!"

"OK, Kelly my dear, we will pick you up at Bangalore station, please be there, and then we can continue to Goa, sure!"

Saturday morning arrives. Kelly is standing at the station waiting for the 09.20 AM train to arrive from Hyderabad. In the distance smoke appears as the over-filled train approaches the station. She spots the boys hanging out of the first-class window, cheering, and smiling. Suddenly she feels like a princess on a magic carpet ride!

"Goa, paradise, I went there once with the love of my life, that is sadly no more, but I cannot wait to join the boys on this wonderful trip to paradise on the Indian Ocean!" She thinks silently.

The train pulls in, Haleem leaps out of the still moving train. He runs towards Kelly with open arms.

"Kelly, darling I missed you so much, how have you been?"

"Haleem, I am fine now, and I just cannot wait to join you and the boys, thank you so much for the invite!"

They hug, he picks up her belongings and they leap happily onto the train which is just about to depart!

Several hours later they arrive in Goa, a pearl on the coast of the Indian ocean once invaded by hippies, John Lennon, George Harrison, and of course the other Beatles. Plus, many other celebrities searching for sobriety, enlightenment, and peace, who adored the place.

A warm Indian Ocean breeze enters the nostrils of the group as they exit the train and head for a local beach hotel booked in advance by Haleem. They walk through the beach market filled with hippies who lost their way many years ago, and remained, among local vendors offering alternative, mostly hand-made products. A colorful, wonderful peaceful paradise. Smells of essence, perfumes and herbs circulate and float on the warm winds entering from the ocean. Palm trees sway and dance to the breezes that give Goa a special 'Bohemian atmosphere', which has been rightly earned over many years; an oasis of 'coolness'.

Kelly feels wonderful as she jaunts along hand in hand with the boys, they enter the hotel and head for the bar!

"Beers on me," Haleem calls!

Who can refuse the offer?

They sit around a huge wooden table on the terrace outside in the wonderful, warm fresh air. The beers flow and then a wonderful evening meal is served. They look out to the ocean, and all agree,

"Wow, this is going to be a great weekend!"

Midnight approaches. Kelly feeling tired after the long journey, decides to retire leaving the boys to enjoy the rest of the night.

Kelly is woken early by the sound of waves caressing the pristine yellow sands, and not feeling too hung-over, she decides to walk barefoot to the beach where she sits alone enjoying the sun rise that gradually releases rays of warmth across the area. Thankfully, the cooling sea breeze takes away the stifling heat that smothers huge cities in India. Here in Goa the heat is bearable, pleasant, and quite wonderful.

Haleem calls from his balcony,

"Kelly, darling breakfast is served, and I am starving!"

She waves and virtually dances back to the hotel terrace, where a wonderful Indian breakfast is served. The other boys join them, they laugh, joke, and lap up the whole Goa atmosphere, and each other's company.

All day long they spend on the beach, swimming, fooling around, eating ice-creams; general things that people do whilst visiting Goa. Kelly feels quite at home with the boys, she just loves Haleem's friends' company and is determined nothing will disturb the wonderful atmosphere; just great friends having a great time!

Day turns into evening, Saturday evening. They all dress and go to the local pub disco and dance until Kelly notices the sun dropping in the west. She wanders outside, onto the beach and plonks herself down facing westwards. The huge red ball that provides us with life sits hovering on the horizon waiting to disappear for another day. Kelly sits mesmerized by the beautiful scene of perfect nature being acted out in front of her eyes. A few passing, fluffy clouds, bathed in deep red reflections from the sun, hang majestically in the pristine sky surrounding the magnificent ball of fire as it gradually drops below the Indian Ocean. Red sparkling sunbeams dance and light up the oceans' surface and, the only thing that Kelly hears is a gentle rustling of coconut tree leaves swaying to the music caused by gentle breezes floating past.

A tear drops down her cheek. She feels emotional as Mother Nature performs one of her greatest acts. Kelly is entwined between feelings of great happiness and sadness as the majestic sun gradually disappears.

Footsteps approach from behind, crunching the pristine sand created over thousands or even millions of years in this paradise. She doesn't look to see who it is but feels the presence of her beloved friend.

He sits beside her,

"Kelly darling, why do you sit here all alone and why is that teardrop running down your cheek? I thought I was going to give you great pleasure this weekend, and now you sit here crying, what is the matter?" Haleem asks gently.

"Haleem, this has nothing to do with you and the boys, it's a personal thing, and when I see the sun disappear in the west, I have a longing to be with my family; my brothers, Sam, Vincent, and Dylan, my mum and dad, Liz and Tanja, and of course Emma, my niece and other family members who live in the west. I feel as if the sun is tugging my feelings apart. I love it here in India, you guys are my adopted brothers, you treat me wonderfully and I want to stay among you. But my family is longing for me to return to my nest and that is why such a beautiful sunset makes me feel emotional, do you understand?"

"Kelly my dear, naturally I understand your dichotomy of feelings. I too have the same problem; loving my family but being driven by my ambitions is also very difficult. You, Kelly, have been a great inspiration to me and the boys. You have fought your terrible illness, you go out against the odds to save stray dogs here in India and, have lost the love of your life. Your incredible will to succeed gives people who surround you, strength. A strength that is invisible and meeting you has given me even more strength; the will to succeed in the face of adversity, prejudice, hate, and discrimination. We love you Kelly like our own sister, but we also understand that your real family loves you too and wants you nearby. This is a decision that only you can take. However, dear Kelly, I can assure you of one thing, wherever your heart takes you we will always be there for you!"

"Oh Haleem, you are so wonderful, you have so much talent and one day will conquer the world that I know. Meeting you and the boys has given me even more hope that one day my life will settle down somewhere and everything will click into place, but for now enough of these emotional outpourings, let's party!!"

They hug and kiss each other on the cheek, both elated that they have found one another, support one another and, most of all, party with each other (LOL)!

They return to the others who by now are dancing on the tables. Kelly, and Haleem, join the fun as their deep-felt emotions are buried in a party rush with some minor drops of the local brew!

Such strong emotions are to be dealt with in the future, but not now because one must fight for the right to party (Thank you Beastie Boys for that one)!

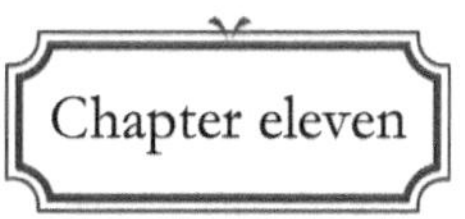

Haleem's dream becomes reality

After a fantastic weekend in Goa, Haleem, attends the meeting organized for him at Telegu head office where all main functionaries are present including the CEO himself. They go through the formal greeting process as Haleem takes his place in the middle of a huge, round, teak table, left behind by superior officers of the British Raj. In fact, the head office of the Telegu group is situated in a huge Victorian mansion once built for high-ranking British officers in Hyderabad; quite impressive, sure!

Haleem signs his contract, the directors' applause as they know they are welcoming one of the hottest properties to their portfolio of top talents already embracing their books. After the formalities, Haleem, is shown around the huge complex embedded in wonderful gardens of exotic trees, bushes, and brightly colored orchids.

A huge, impressive film studio has been erected in one corner of the complex, plus other studios for dance, theater, opera, and classical dance, which stand proudly between wonderful, landscaped gardens.

"A perfect place to develop my skills," Haleem thinks silently smiling as a crew of high-level directors proudly show him his new place of work.

"Haleem, dear boy, do you like our home?"

"Sir, it is wonderful, and I feel at home already!"

"We are also grateful to have you among us and may we spend many happy years together, I know we will!" The CEO answers.

"Sure Sire, sure!"

Several years pass, and after more than 800 solo, and group performances under the guidance of his 'guru', Shri Kaza Venkata Subramanyam garu, all over India, Haleem continues to wow and mesmerize audiences during performances of Kuchipudi classical dance routines. Haleem's meteoric career reaches, and touches thousands live on stage and Indian main-stream television He also appears in many Telegu film productions.

One highlight of his career is an invitation to go to the USA as a guest of The American Telegu Association in Minnesota where he performs and gives Kuchipudi workshops to budding Indian talents born in America determined to keep ancient Indian culture and traditions alive in their new homeland.

Among his many appearances in Hyderabad is a fantastic live performance in the Russian Art Theater normally reserved for prestigious Russian ballet groups visiting the country. He wows them there too!

Live national TV, films, and theatre, become his life and, after all the initial struggles and battles, especially with his father, Haleem Khan proves to many budding, talented people from diverse ethnic and religious backgrounds; success can be achieved! In the face of discrimination, sexual and religious, prejudice, antiquated religious incarceration, homophobic morons and others who just cannot accept that the world is not quite so normal as they believe they are; Haleem Khan proves them all wrong!

Only those truly dedicated and strong achieve their goals,
Haleem Khan is proof of that!

Resumé

Although this quite unbelievable story is only based upon the real-life of Haleem Khan, there are many parts which are true, especially his conflicts with ignorance, discrimination, and prejudice. Having a Muslim background has been especially difficult due to the fact he performs many times as a female dancer and, this is hard to accept for the Muslim fraternity, especially in India. I have obviously added many fictive scenarios and characters to the story. However, these scenarios occur daily all over the planet as majorities continue to discriminate, exclude and, hate minorities that are different from the rest.

It matters not from which ethnic background we come from, which color our skin is, which religion or God we believe in, or which sexual preference we practice; we all belong to one race, the human race, an imperfect race. This imperfect race continues to murder, kill, hate, discriminate, respect and love, the great paradox and division.

However, it is not enough that only the enlightened ones among us practice the last two, respect and love. The whole human race must learn to accept fundamental differences, respect those differences and, allow those who are different, or believe different, to exist in a humane manner. A Utopian ideal maybe, but I am convinced people who read the story of

Haleem Khan will be moved by his determination to bridge those gaps with hard work, love, and respect. I sincerely hope the reader will return the favor to those with similar backgrounds to Haleem Khan.

L.R. Johnson

Just to complete the story based upon Haleem's life, here are some images of the 'real' person.

I have thoroughly enjoyed writing this book, although the information I received from Haleem was very sparse, but never mind, the book is as close as I could get without being a biographical, true story!

Cover for an Indian National Press interview

A male Super Star in the Kuchipudi dance world!

Acting, another passion of Haleem's

Teaching others and breaking down barriers!

In full flow!

Film promotion!

To Dance or Not to Dance? This is not the Question | 111

The man himself!

A demanding role!

We wish the 'Real Haleem Khan' all the very best for the future!